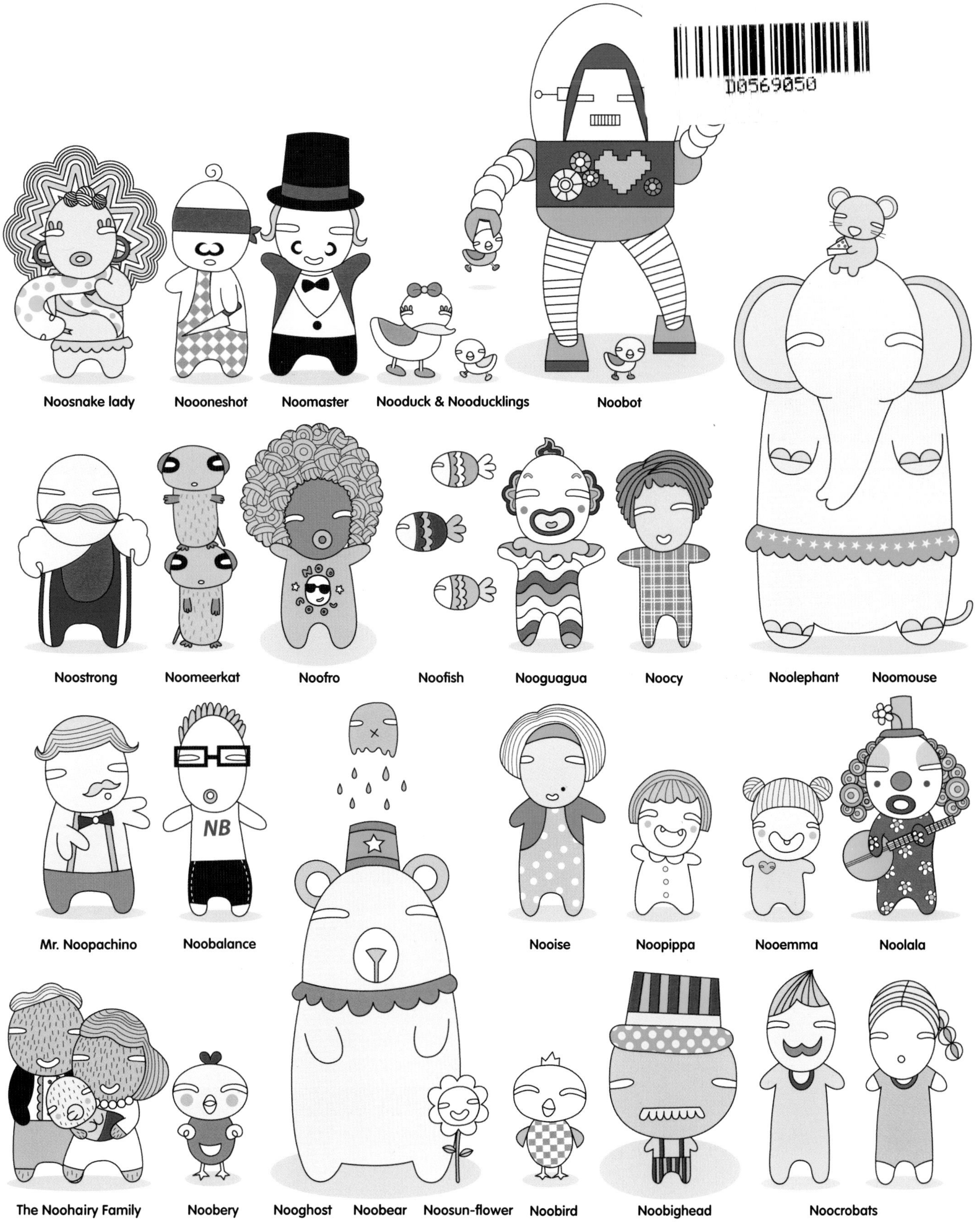
Noosnake lady
Noooneshot
Noomaster
Nooduck & Nooducklings
Noobot
Noostrong
Noomeerkat
Noofro
Noofish
Nooguagua
Noocy
Noolephant
Noomouse
Mr. Noopachino
Noobalance
Nooise
Noopippa
Nooemma
Noolala
The Noohairy Family
Noobery
Nooghost
Noobear
Noosun-flower
Noobird
Noobighead
Noocrobats

Copyright © 2009 by YiYing Wang
All rights reserved
CIP Data is available
Published in the United States in 2009 by
🍎 Blue Apple Books
515 Valley Street, Maplewood, NJ 07040
www.blueapplebooks.com

Distributed in the U.S. by Chronicle Books
First Edition
Printed in China

ISBN: 978-1-934706-49-7

1  3  5  7  9  10  8  6  4  2

NOODOLL studio

I ♥ Noo

www.noodoll.com

Hiya

LUKE

Special thanks to
Luke James
for his contribution
to Noodletown

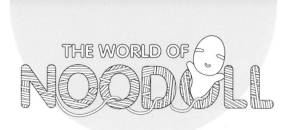

# THE WORLD OF NOODOLL

BY YiYing Wang

# Ricehead's REVENGE!

🍎 BLUE APPLE BOOKS

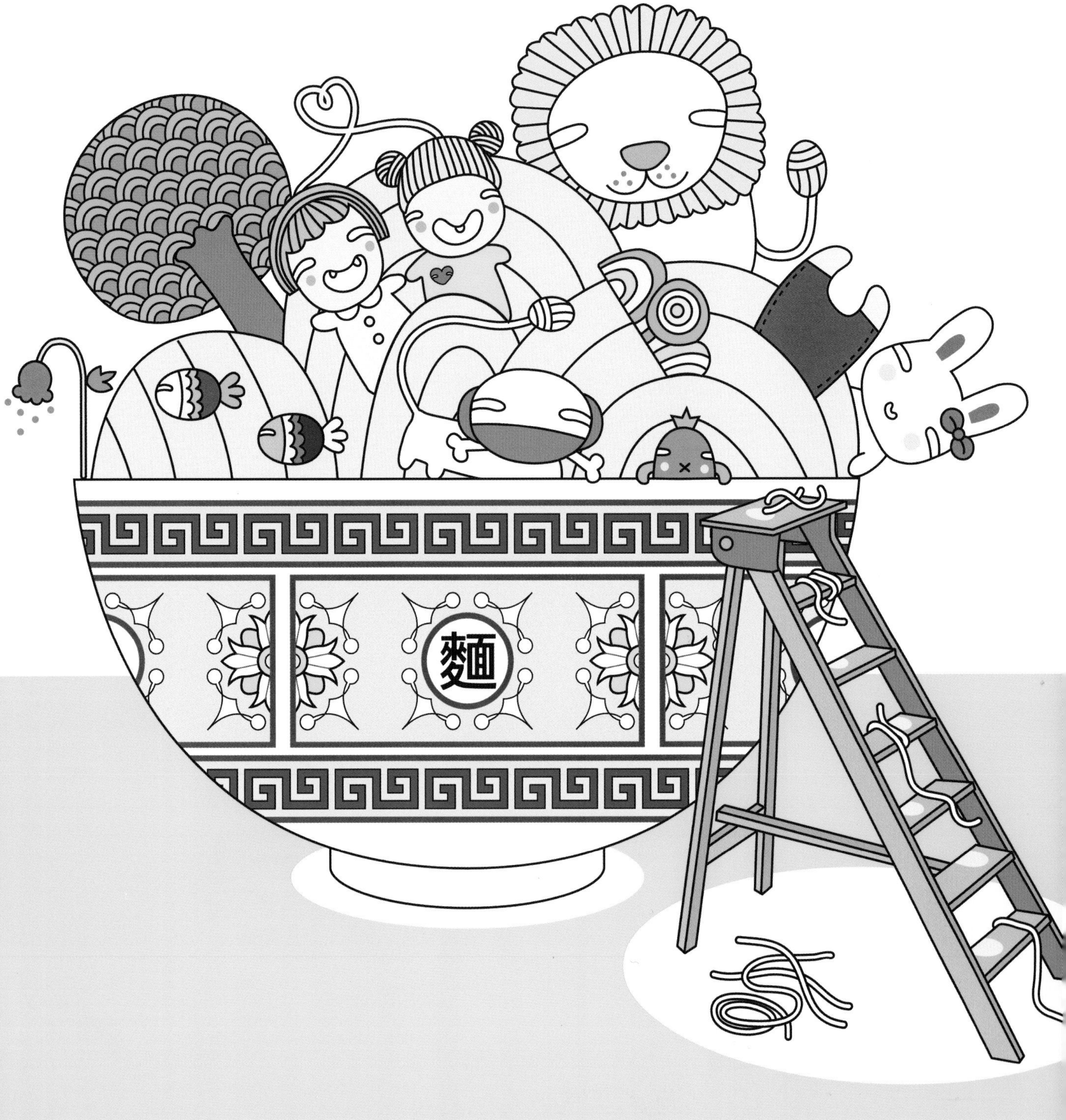
麵

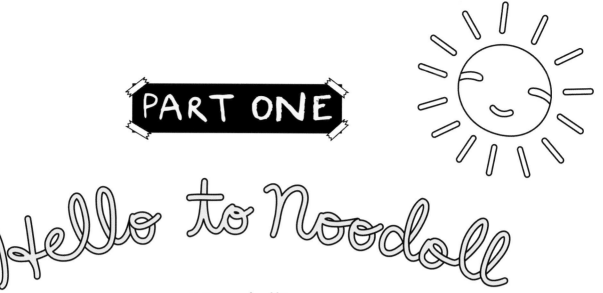

# PART ONE

# Hello to Noodoll

**Noodoll's
from a special land:**

Hello, everyone!

**Noodletown,
it's truly grand.**

Everything is made of noodles.

Houses, people . . .

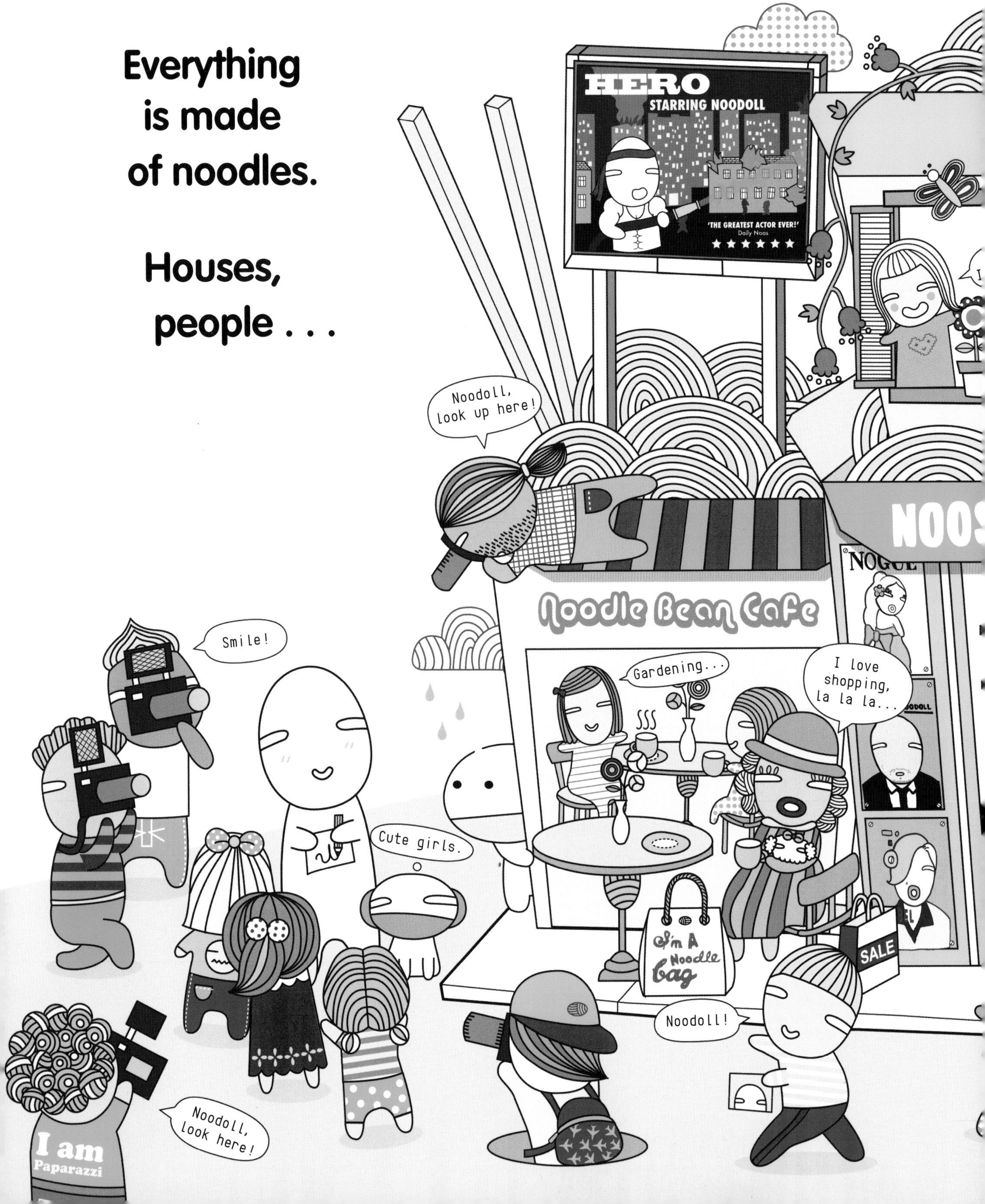
HERO
STARRING NOODOLL
'THE GREATEST ACTOR EVER!'
Daily Noos
Noodoll, look up here!
NOGUE
Noodle Bean Cafe
Smile!
Gardening...
I love shopping, la la la...
Cute girls.
I'm A Noodle bag
SALE
Noodoll!
Noodoll, look here!
I am Paparazzi

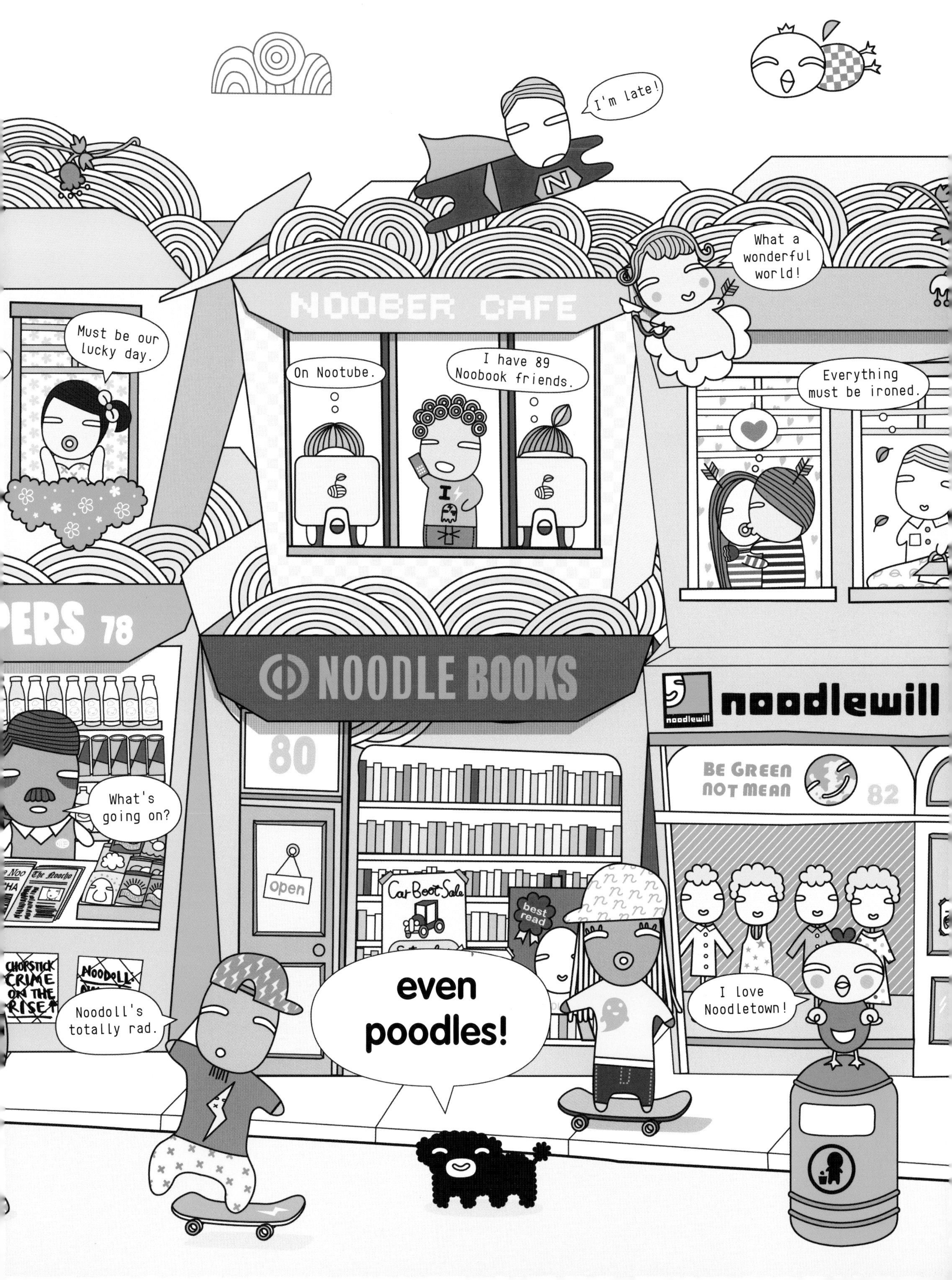
I'm late!
What a wonderful world!
NOOBER CAFE
Must be our lucky day.
On Nootube.
I have 89 Noobook friends.
Everything must be ironed.
PERS 78
NOODLE BOOKS
noodlewill
BE GREEN NOT MEAN
82
80
What's going on?
open
Car Boot Sale
best read
CHOPSTICK CRIME ON THE RISE
Noodoll's totally rad.
even poodles!
I love Noodletown!

Noodoll's famous near and far.

He is Noodletown's biggest star.

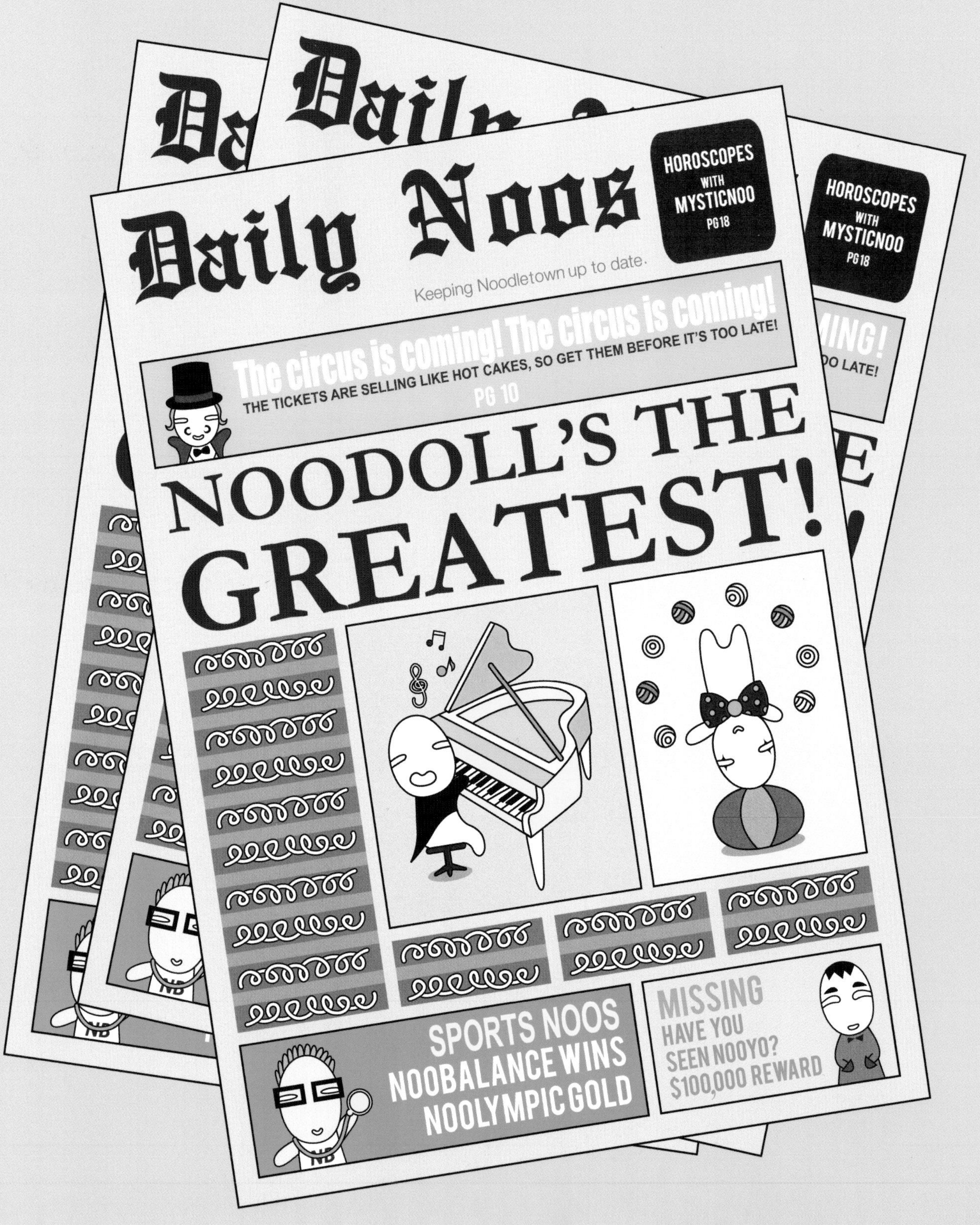

Daily Noos
HOROSCOPES WITH MYSTICNOO PG18
Keeping Noodletown up to date.
The circus is coming! The circus is coming!
THE TICKETS ARE SELLING LIKE HOT CAKES, SO GET THEM BEFORE IT'S TOO LATE!
PG 10
NOODOLL'S THE GREATEST!
SPORTS NOOS
NOOBALANCE WINS NOOLYMPIC GOLD
MISSING
HAVE YOU SEEN NOOYO?
$100,000 REWARD

# PART TWO

# Hello to Ricehead

Ricehead
lives in old Ricetown.

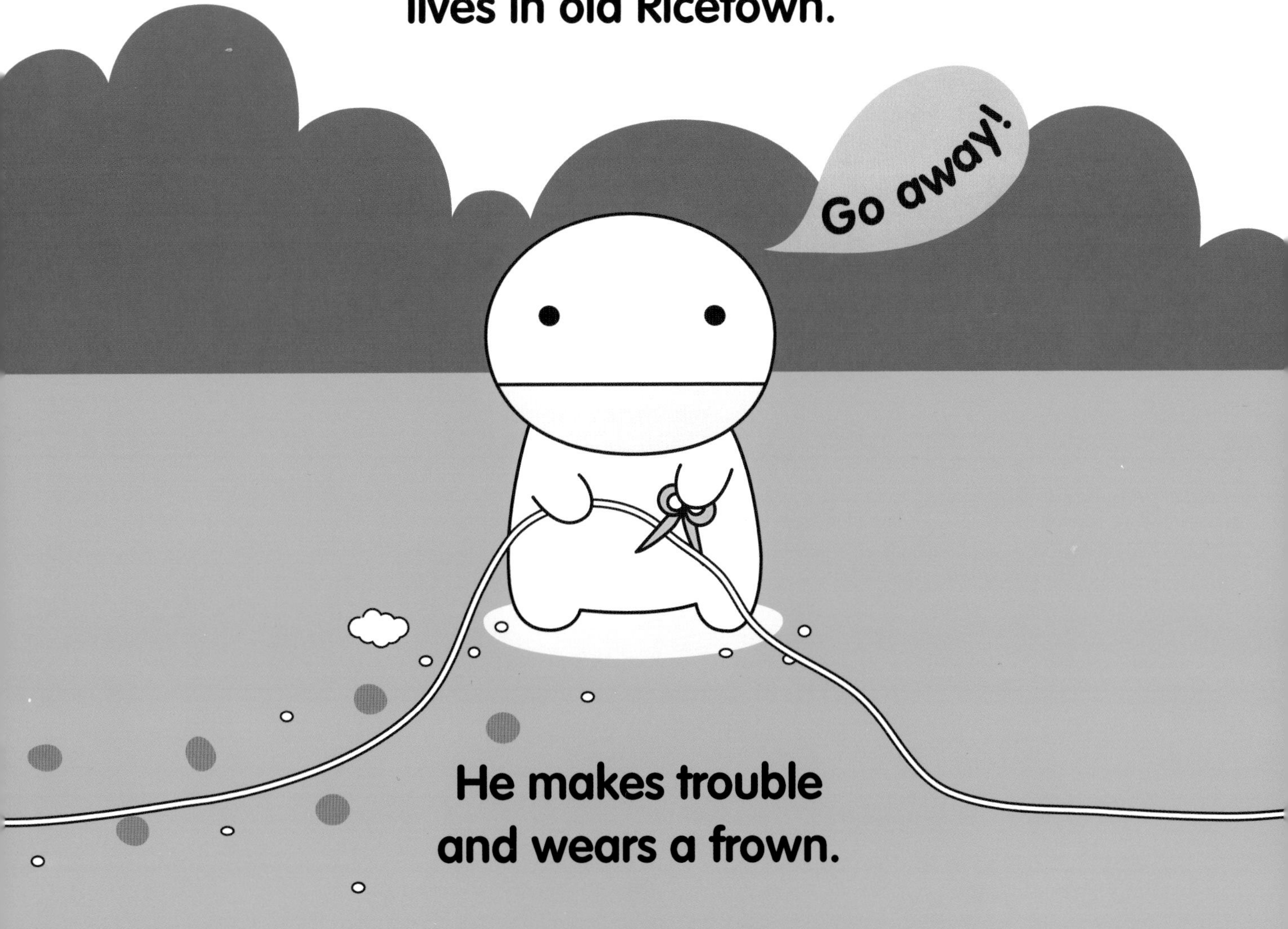
Go away!

He makes trouble
and wears a frown.

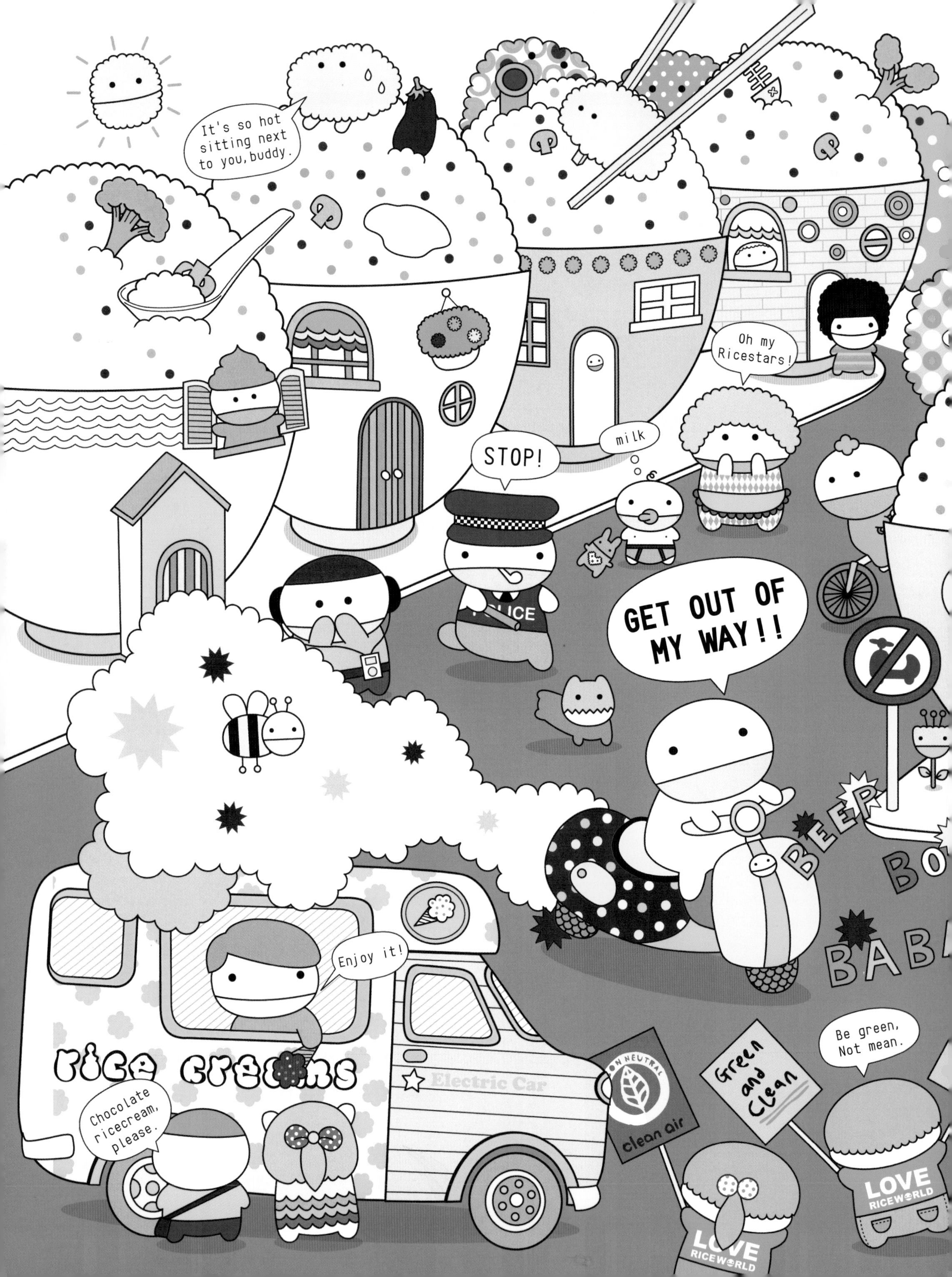

It's so hot sitting next to you, buddy.
Oh my Ricestars!
milk
STOP!
POLICE
GET OUT OF MY WAY!!
BEEP
BO
BAB
Enjoy it!
rice creams
Electric Car
Chocolate ricecream, please.
clean air
Green and Clean
Be green, Not mean.
LOVE RICEWORLD
LOVE RICEWORLD

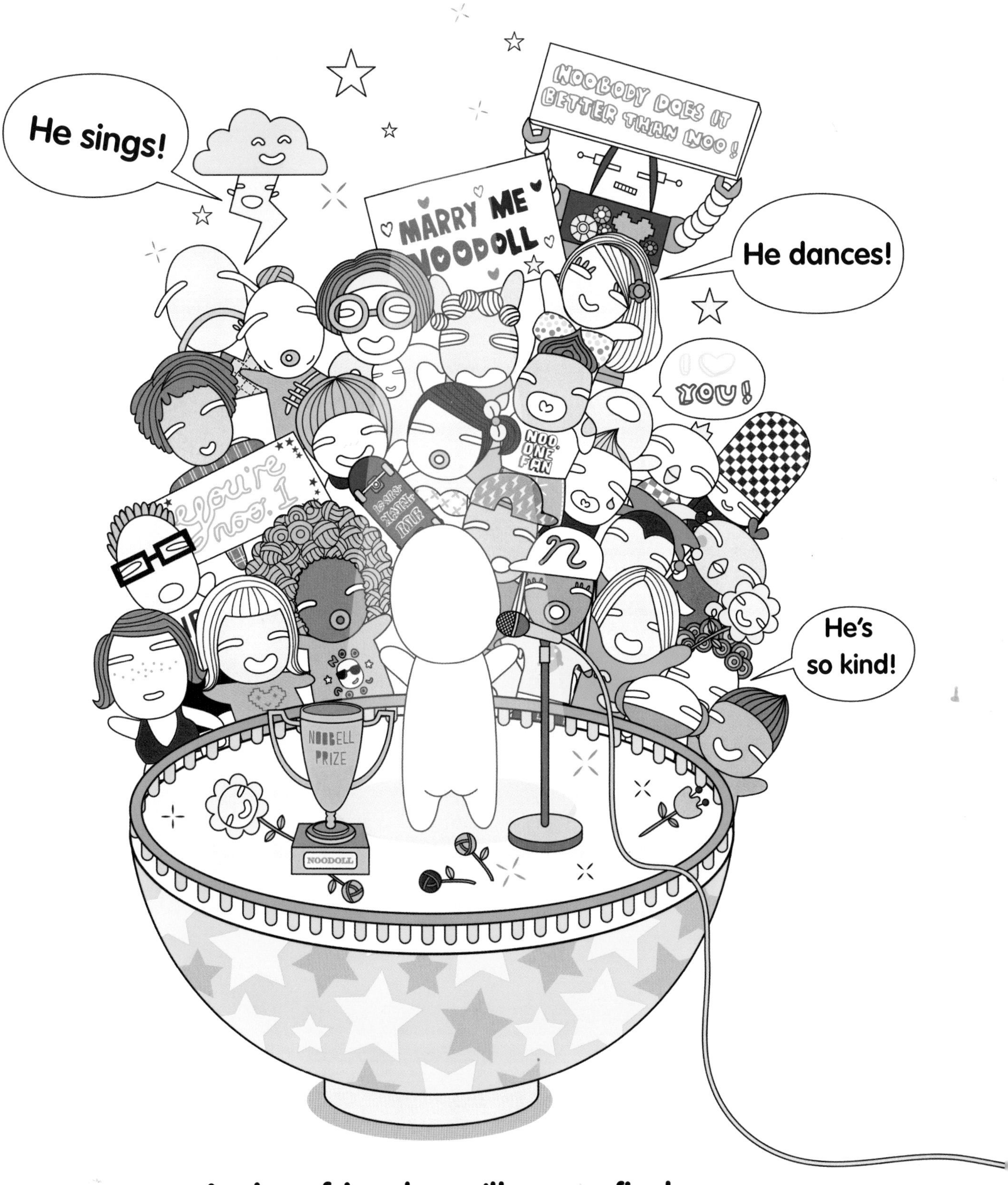
He sings!
NOOBODY DOES IT BETTER THAN NOO !
MARRY ME NOODOLL
He dances!
I YOU !
NOO, ONE FAN
You're noo. 1
NOOBELL PRIZE
NOODOLL
He's so kind!

A nicer friend you'll never find.

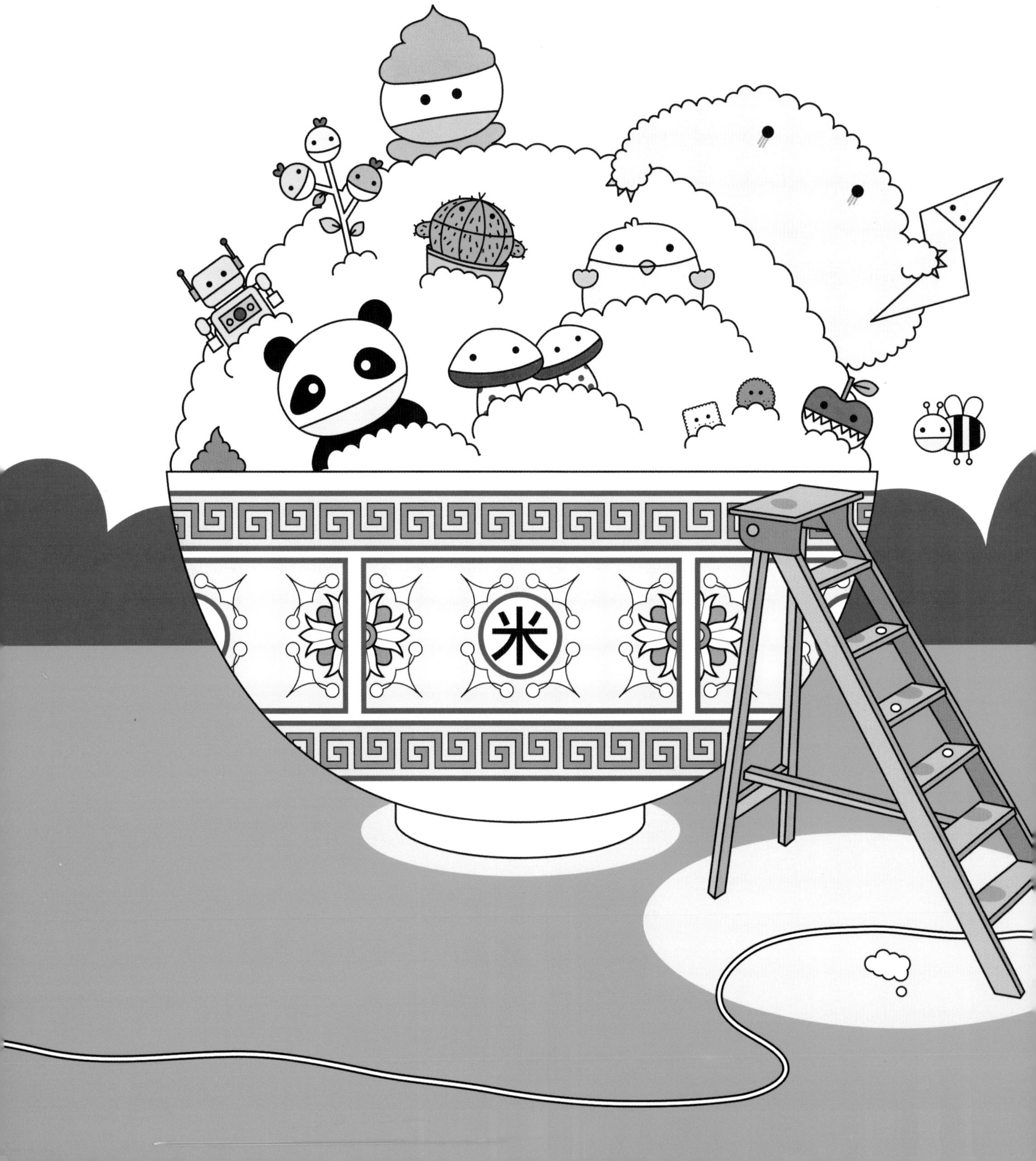
米

**He likes to hide, but when he's seen,**
**Ricehead's nasty and always mean.**

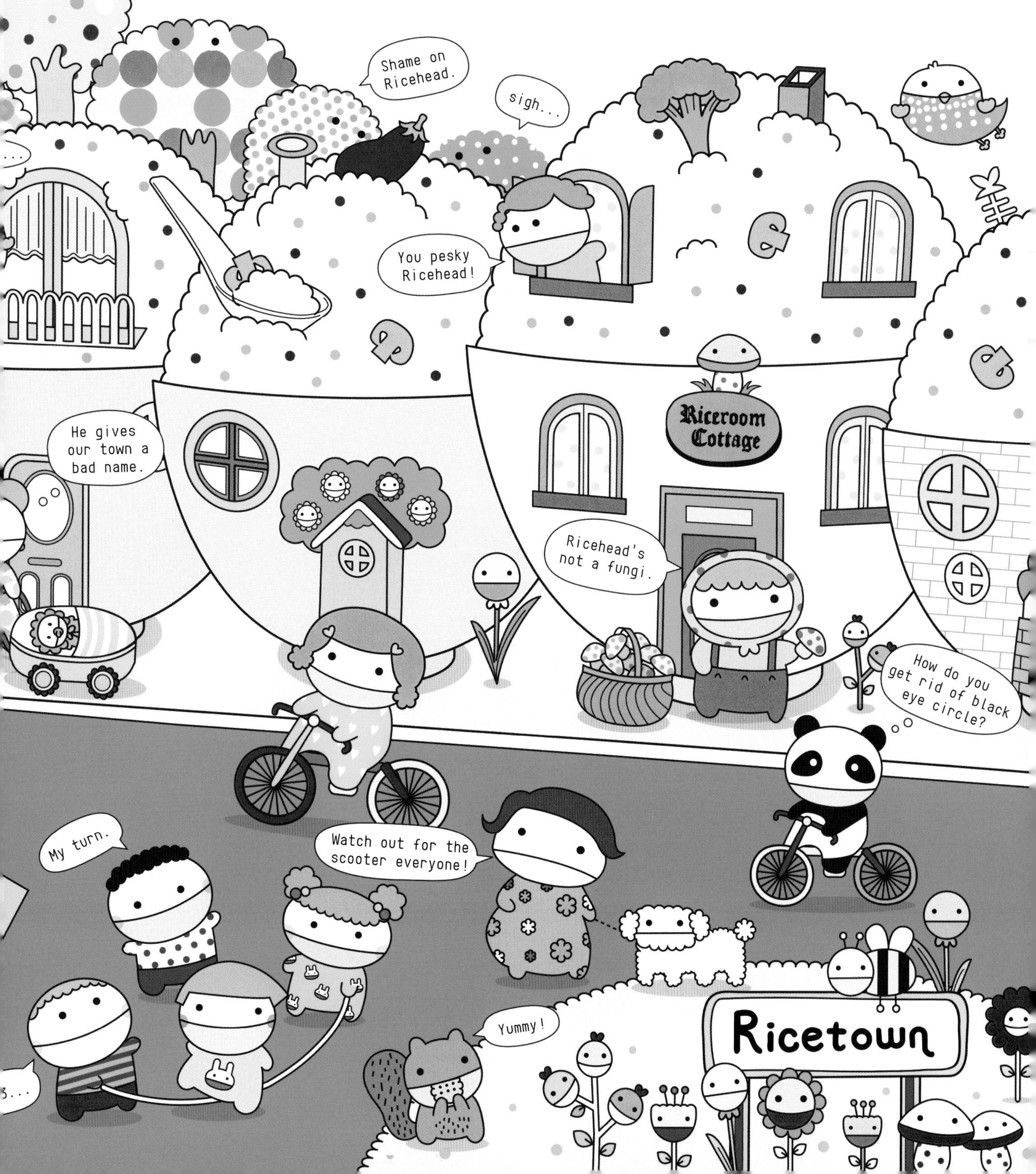
Shame on Ricehead.
sigh...
You pesky Ricehead!
Riceroom Cottage
He gives our town a bad name.
Ricehead's not a fungi.
How do you get rid of black eye circle?
My turn.
Watch out for the scooter everyone!
Yummy!
Ricetown

**Ricehead's jealous of Noodoll's fame.**
**He wishes he could have the same.**

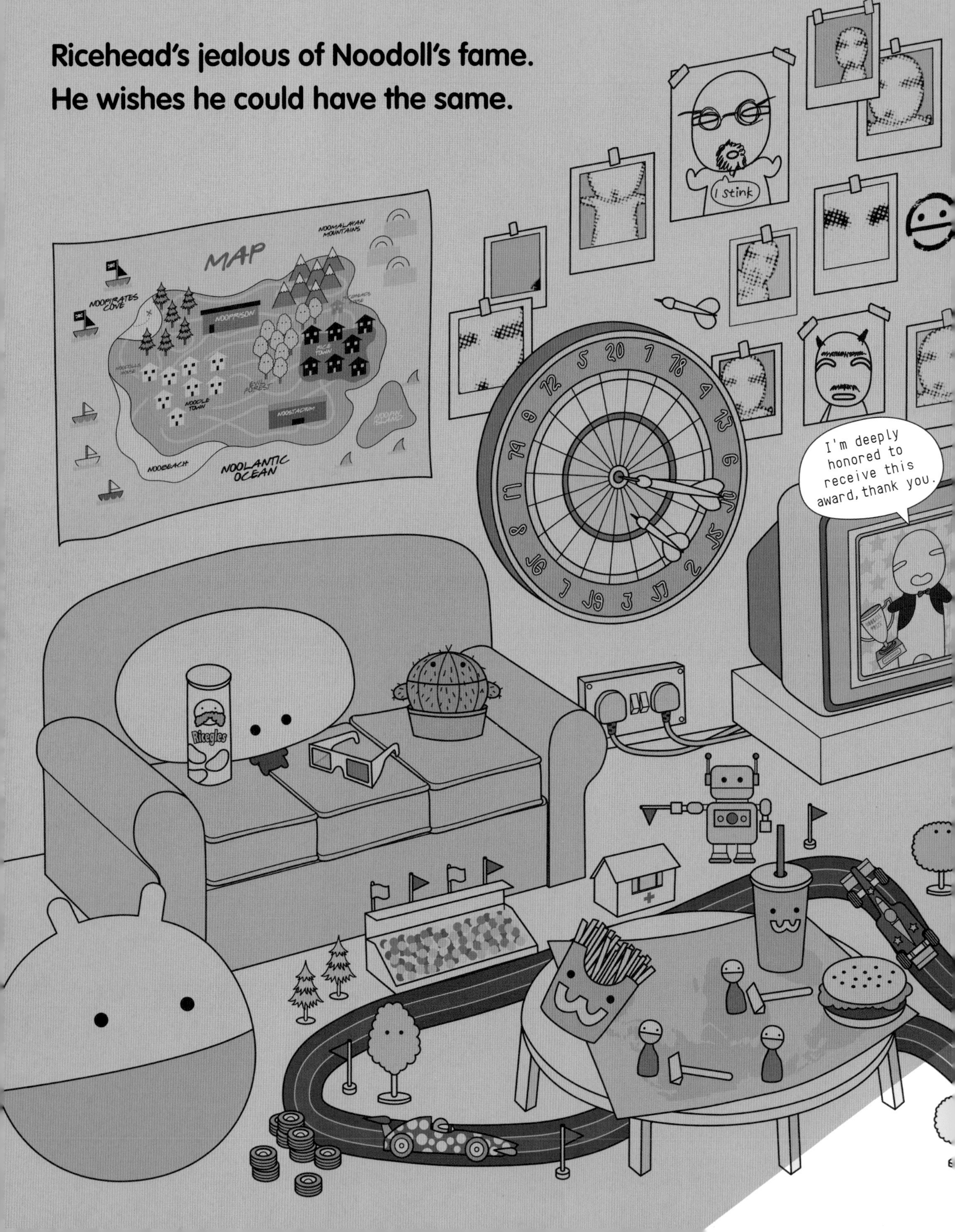
MAP
NOOMALAYAN MOUNTAINS
NOOPIRATES COVE
NOOPRISON
RICE TOWN
NOODLE TOWN
NOOSTADIUM
NOOBEACH
NOOLANTIC OCEAN
I stink
I'm deeply honored to receive this award, thank you.
Riceggles

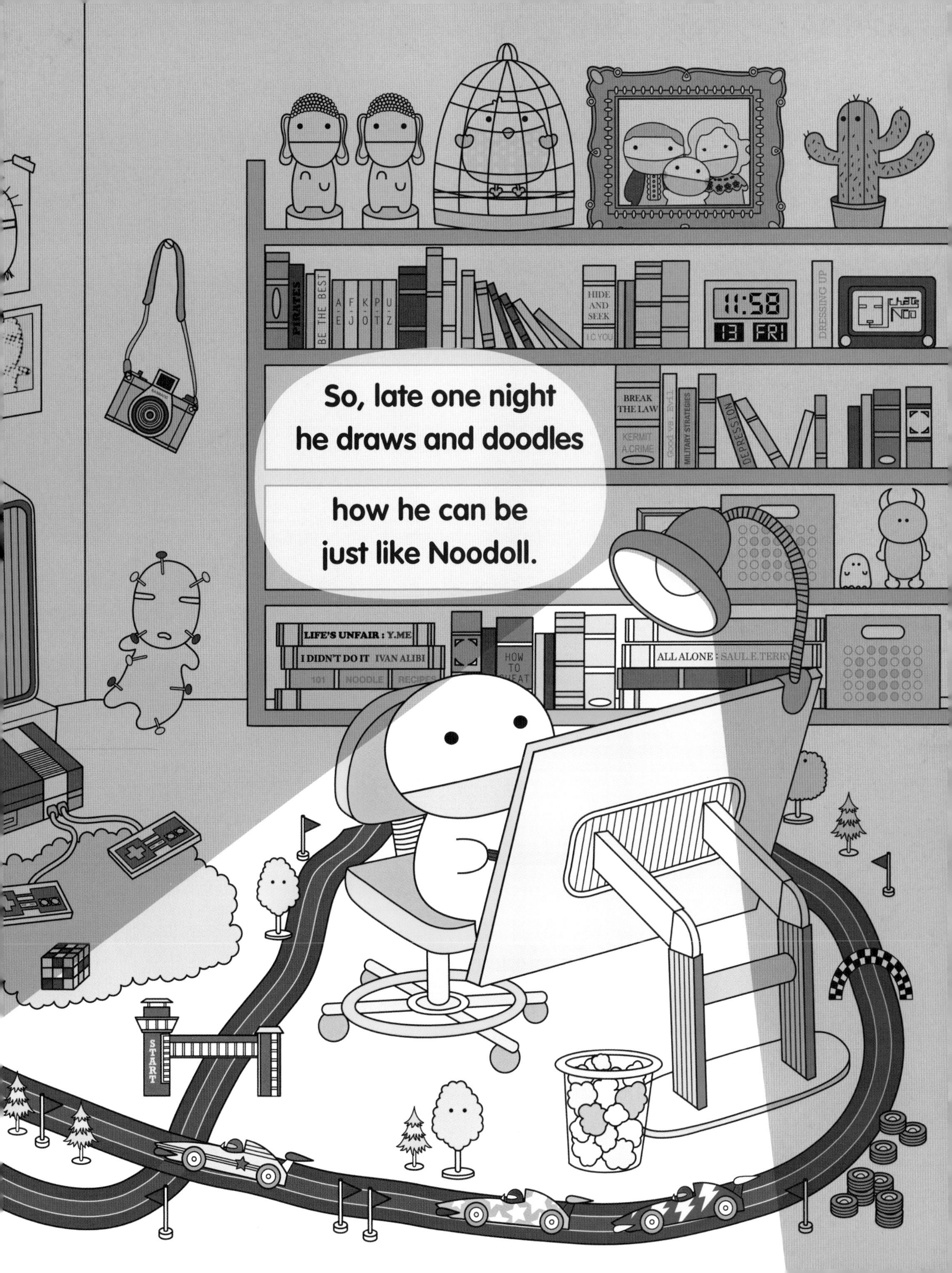
So, late one night
he draws and doodles
how he can be
just like Noodoll.
PIRATES
BE THE BEST
HIDE AND SEEK
I.C.YOU
11:58
13 FRI
DRESSING UP
BREAK THE LAW
KERMIT A.CRIME
Good vs. Evil
MILITARY STRATEGIES
DEPRESSION
LIFE'S UNFAIR : Y.ME
I DIDN'T DO IT IVAN ALIBI
101 NOODLE RECIPES
ALL ALONE : SAUL.E.TERRY
START

# PART THREE

# Ricehead's Plot

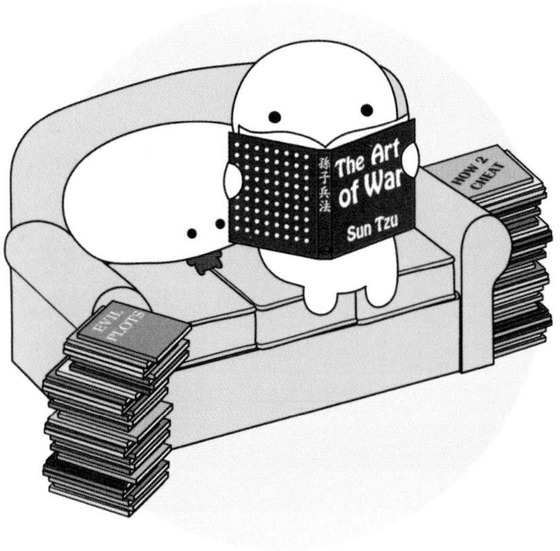

孫子兵法
The Art of War
Sun Tzu
HOW 2 CHEAT
EVIL PLOTS


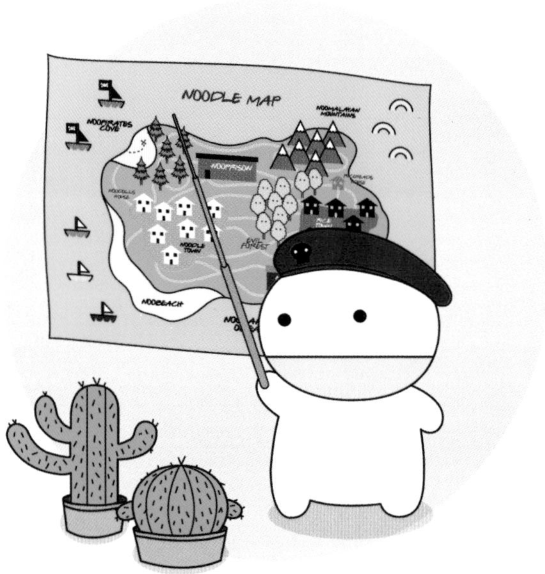

NOODLE MAP
NOOPRISON

**He plans and plots until he's done**
**a way that *he'll* be Number One.**

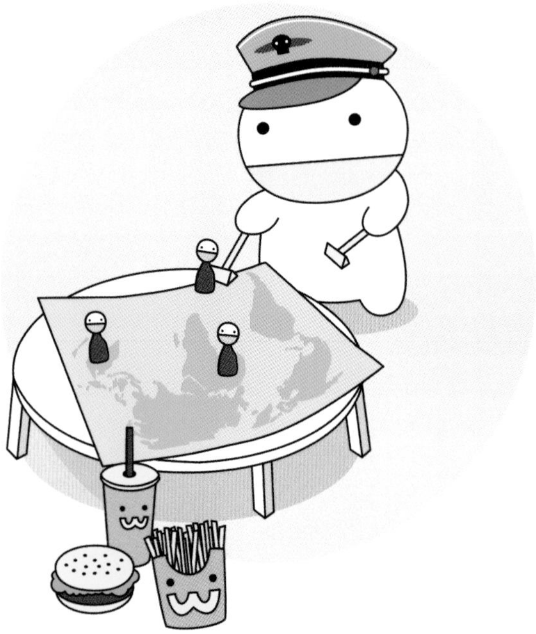

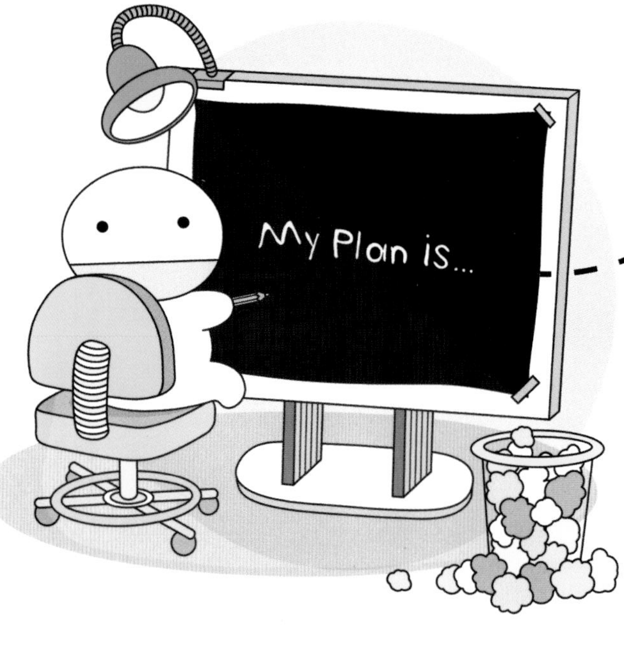

My Plan is...

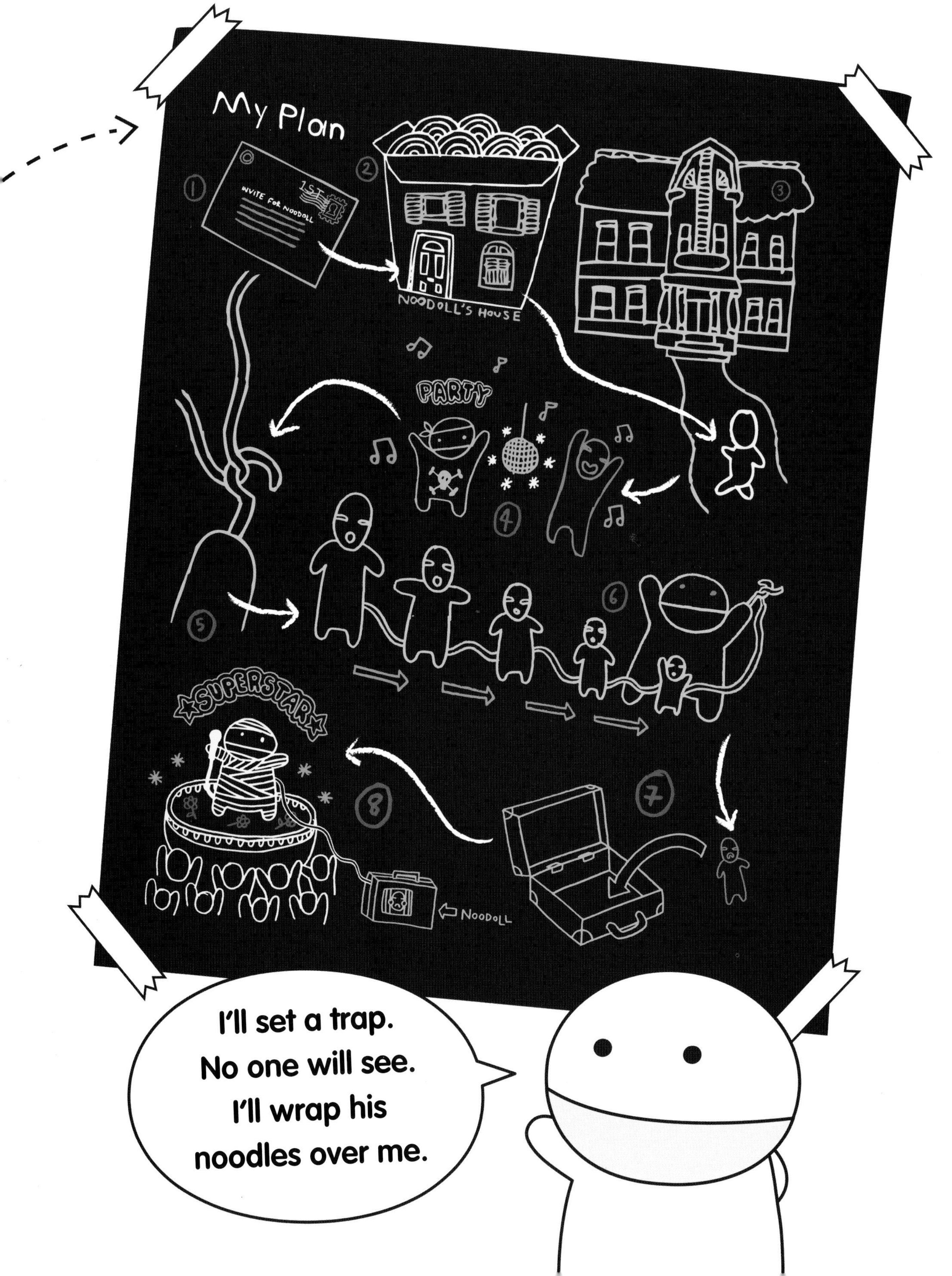

My Plan
INVITE FOR NOODOLL
1ST
NOODOLL'S HOUSE
PARTY
SUPERSTAR
NOODOLL
I'll set a trap.
No one will see.
I'll wrap his
noodles over me.

**Ricehead's plan is a sneaky surprise.**
**He will dress up in disguise.**

**Which of these costumes will be the best**
**to fool Noodoll and the rest?**

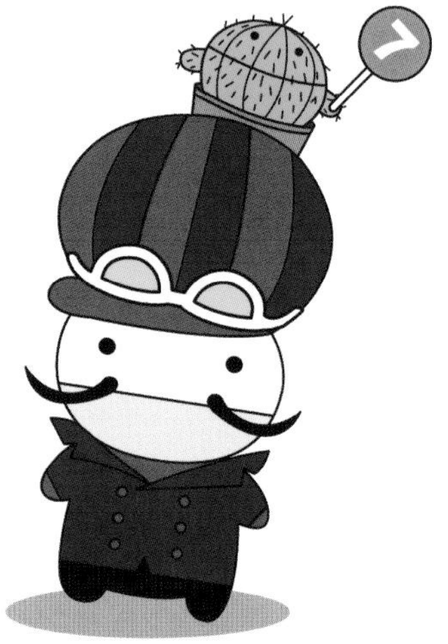

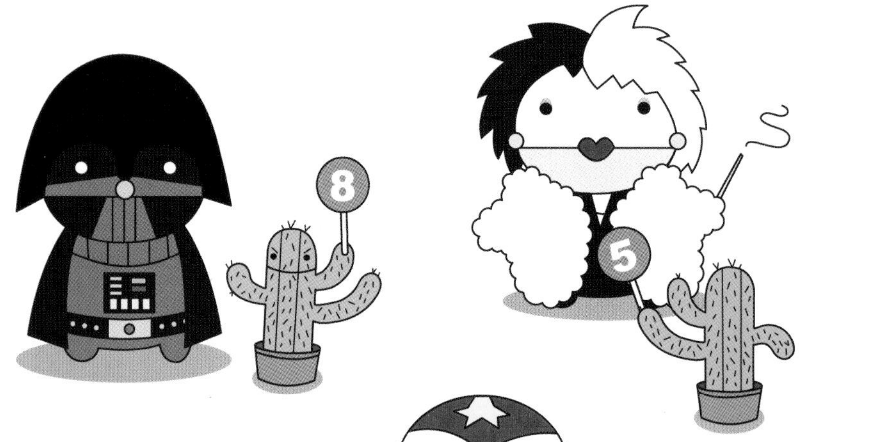

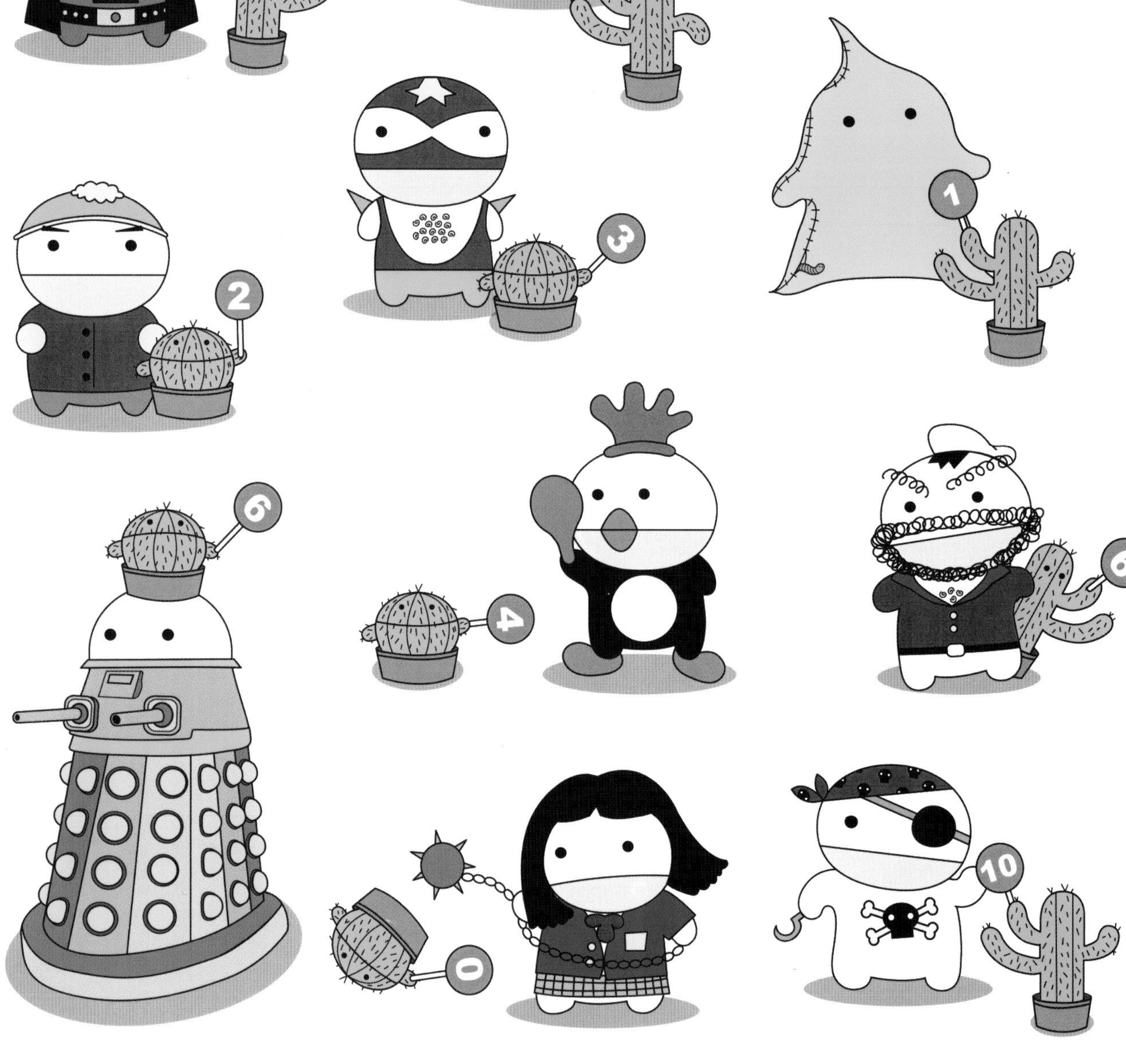

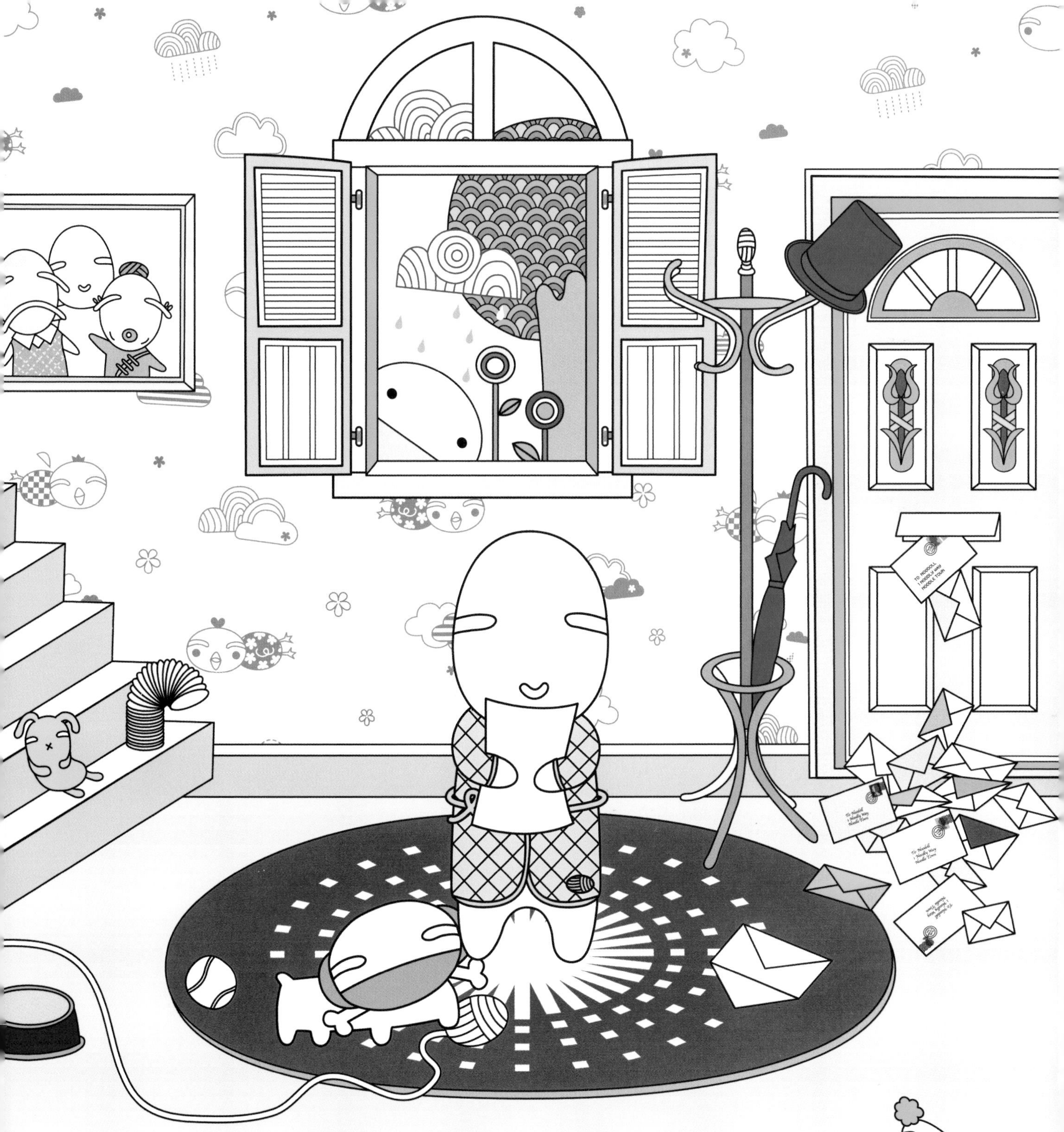

The next morning at ten o'clock
Noodoll hears the postman's knock.

When he finds the invitation,
he is filled with great elation.

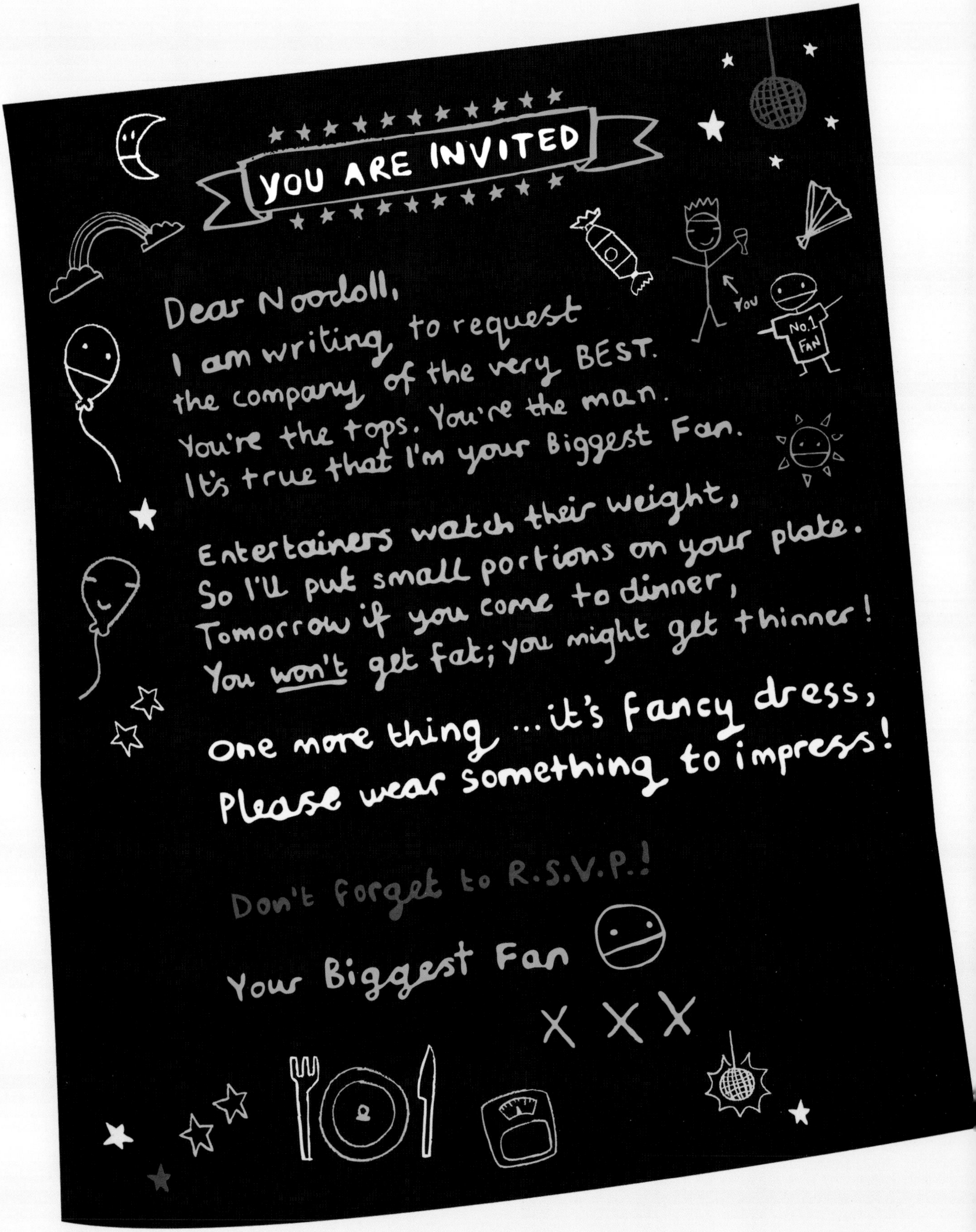

YOU ARE INVITED

Dear Noodoll,
I am writing to request
the company of the very BEST.
You're the tops. You're the man.
It's true that I'm your Biggest Fan.

Entertainers watch their weight,
So I'll put small portions on your plate.
Tomorrow if you come to dinner,
You won't get fat; you might get thinner!

One more thing ... it's fancy dress,
Please wear something to impress!

Don't forget to R.S.V.P.!

Your Biggest Fan

X X X


YOU
No.1 FAN

For tomorrow's celebration,
Noodoll must find a cool creation.

He doesn't suspect Ricehead at all.
Noodoll thinks he'll have a ball.

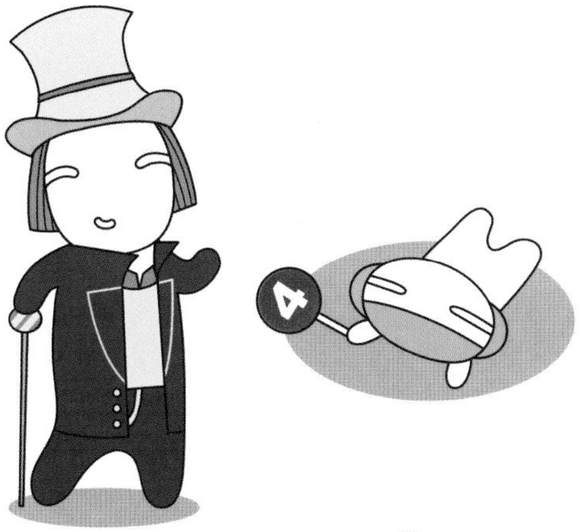
4

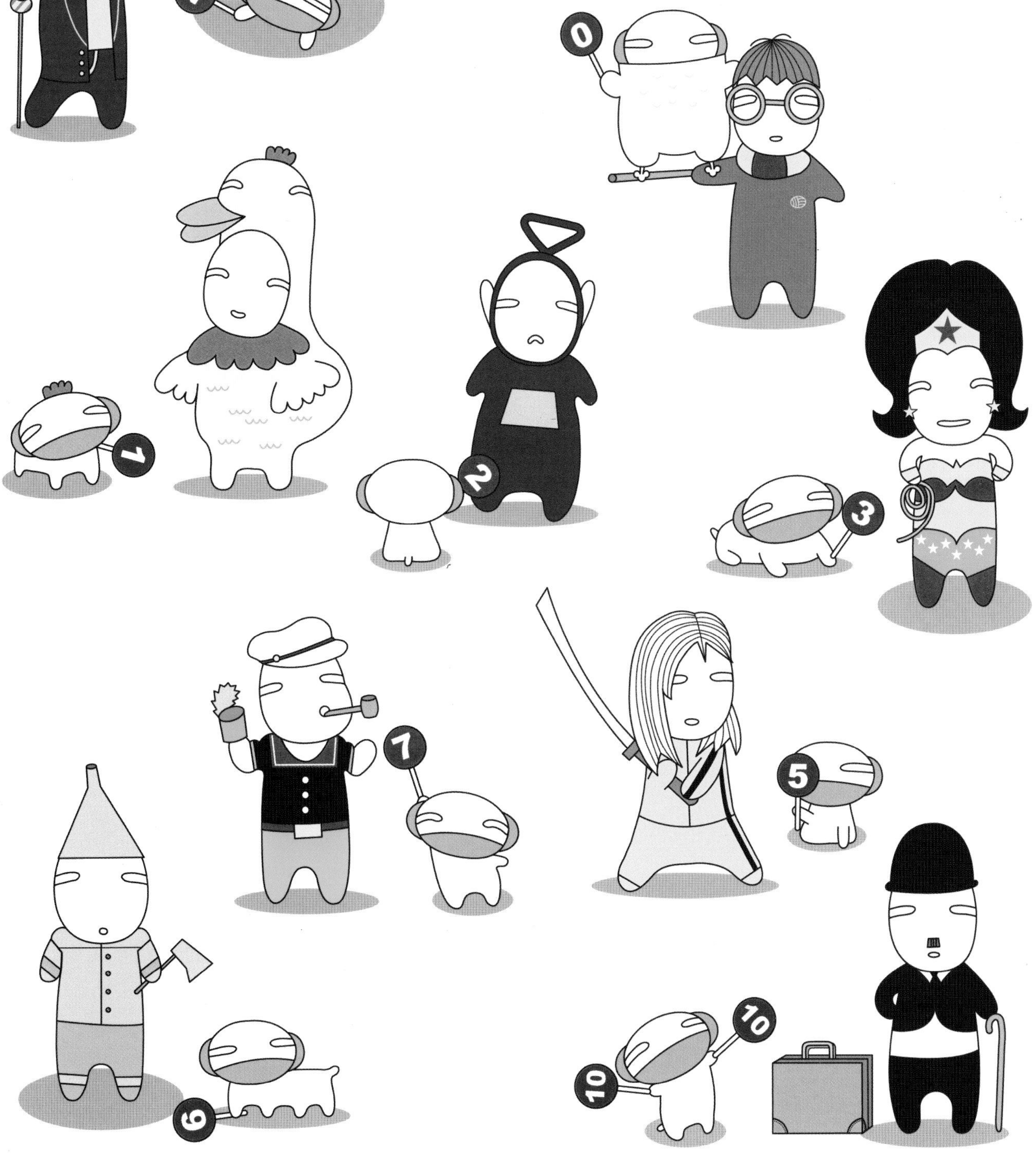
0
1
2
3
7
5
6
10
10

# PART FOUR

# The Party

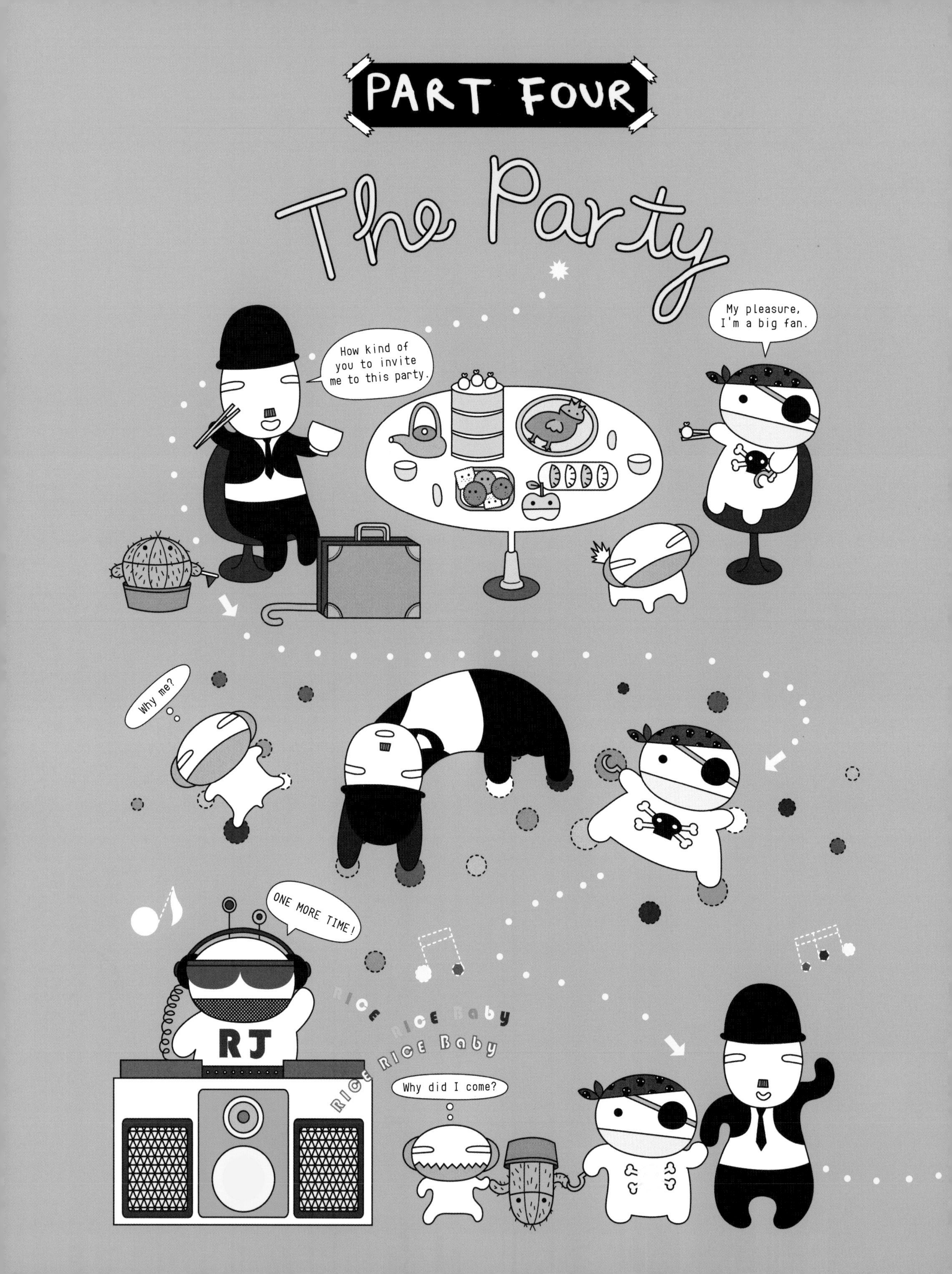
How kind of you to invite me to this party.
My pleasure, I'm a big fan.
Why me?
ONE MORE TIME!
RICE RICE Baby
RICE RICE Baby
Why did I come?
RJ

The fancy party comes at last.
Ricehead and Noodoll have a blast.

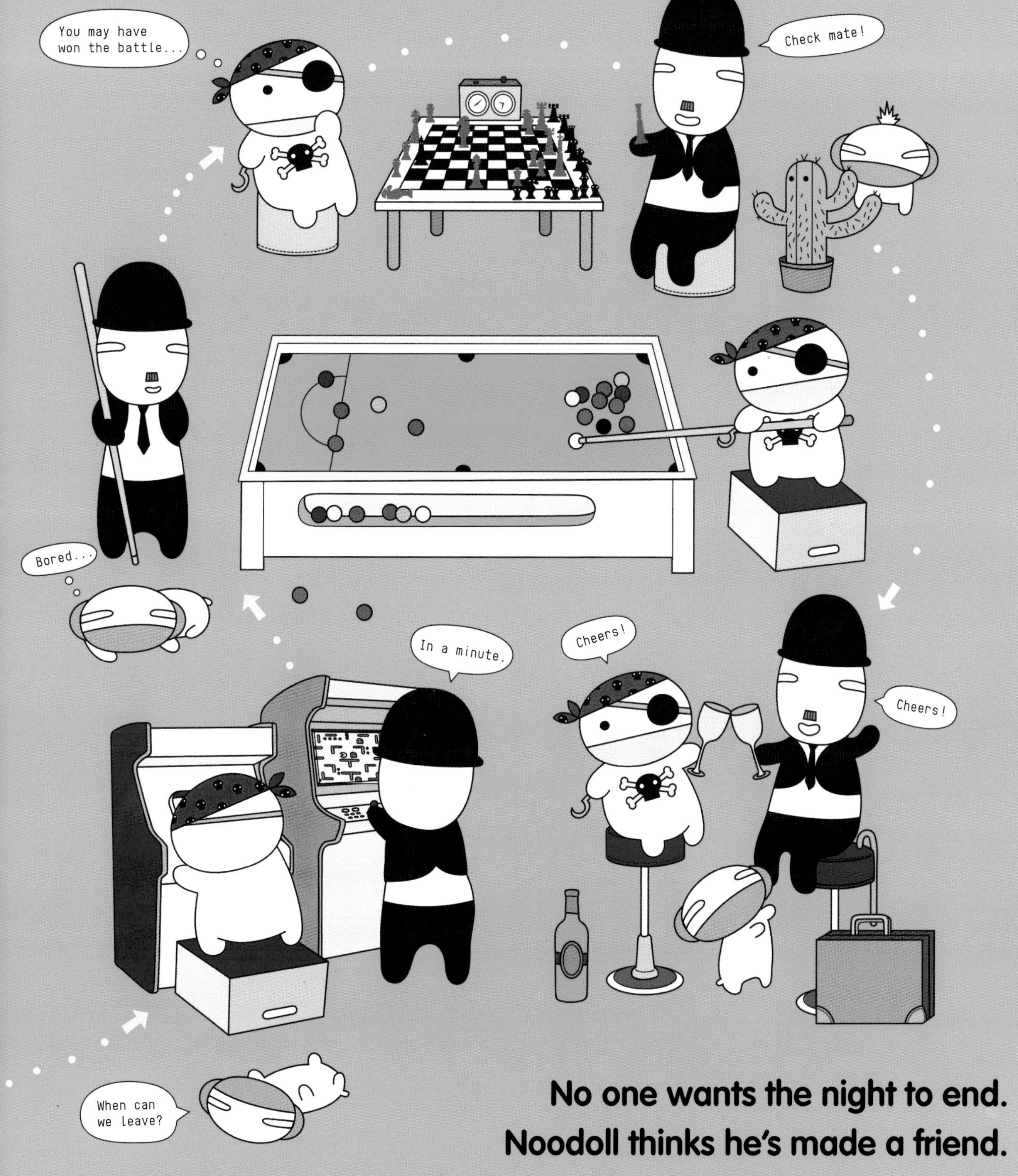
You may have won the battle...
Check mate!
Bored...
In a minute.
Cheers!
Cheers!
When can we leave?

No one wants the night to end.
Noodoll thinks he's made a friend.

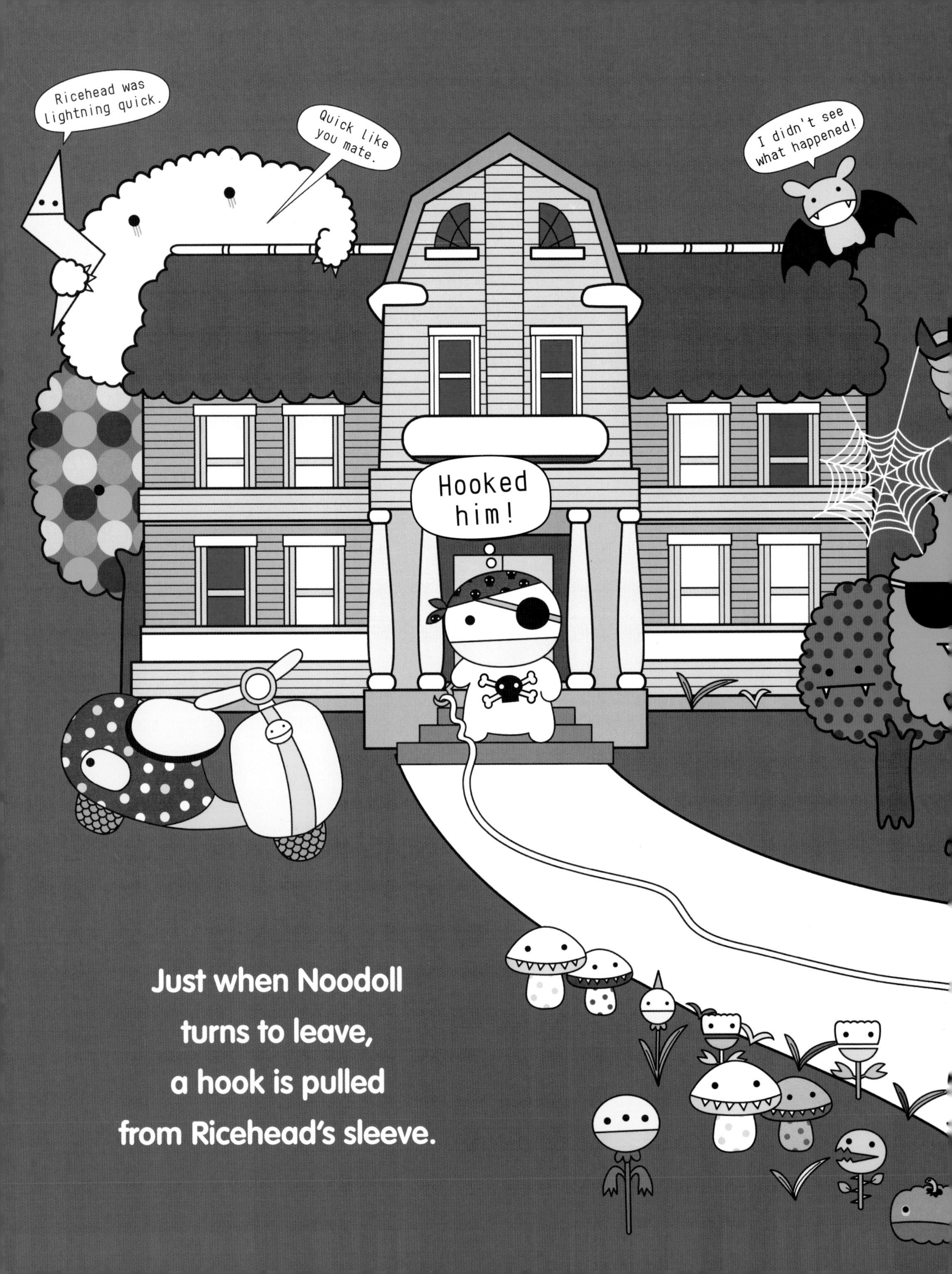
Ricehead was lightning quick.
Quick like you mate.
I didn't see what happened!
Hooked him!

**Just when Noodoll turns to leave, a hook is pulled from Ricehead's sleeve.**

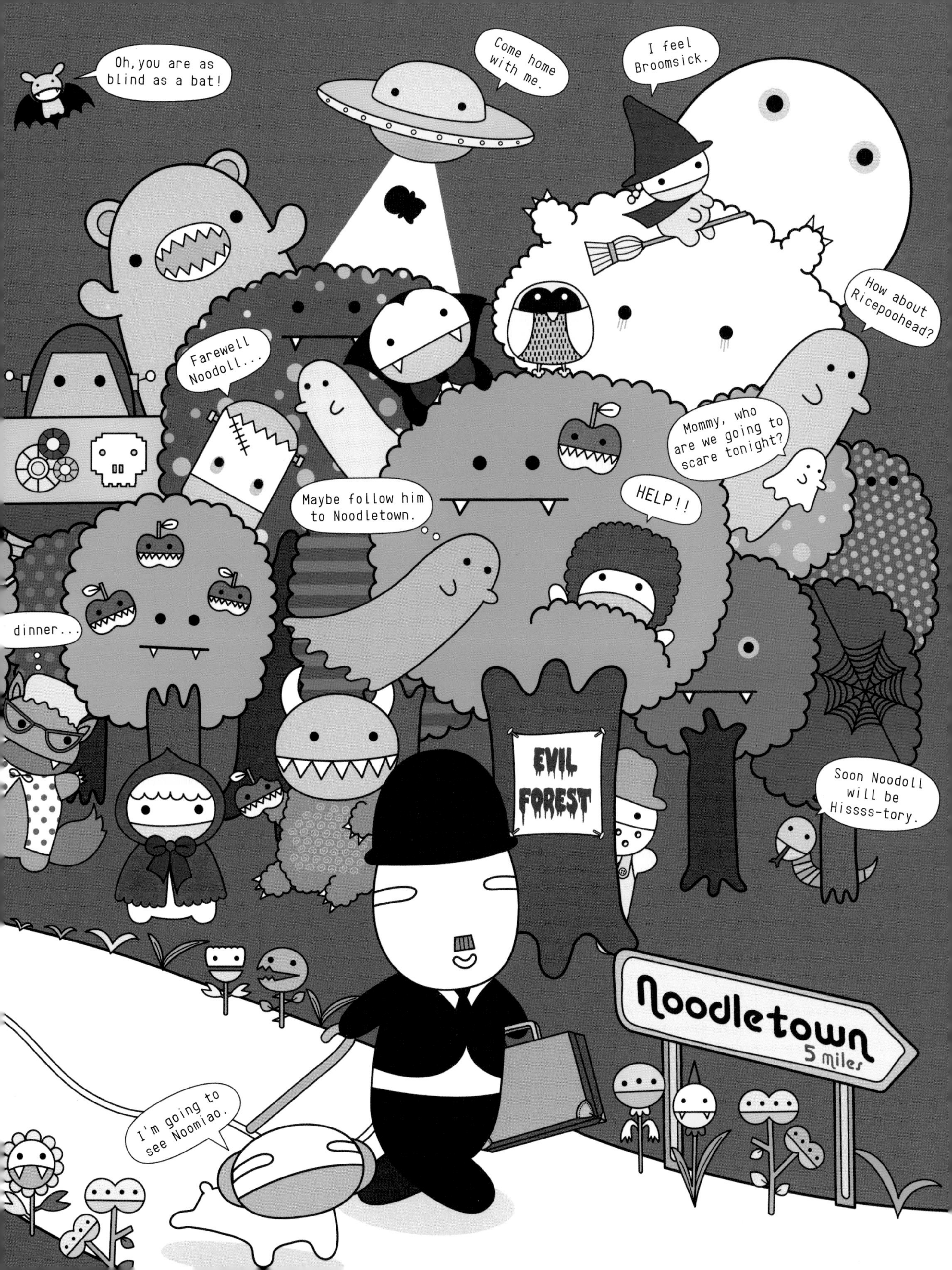
Oh, you are as blind as a bat!
Come home with me.
I feel Broomsick.
How about Ricepoohead?
Farewell Noodoll...
Mommy, who are we going to scare tonight?
Maybe follow him to Noodletown.
HELP!!
dinner...
EVIL FOREST
Soon Noodoll will be Hissss-tory.
Noodletown
5 miles
I'm going to see Noomiao.

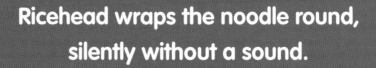

Ricehead wraps the noodle round,
silently without a sound.

I'm
shrinking!

I am the
NEW
Noodoll!

Smaller, smaller Noodoll grows
from his head down to his toes.

What's
happening
to me?

Ricehead hides him in a box.
He shuts it tight with seven locks.

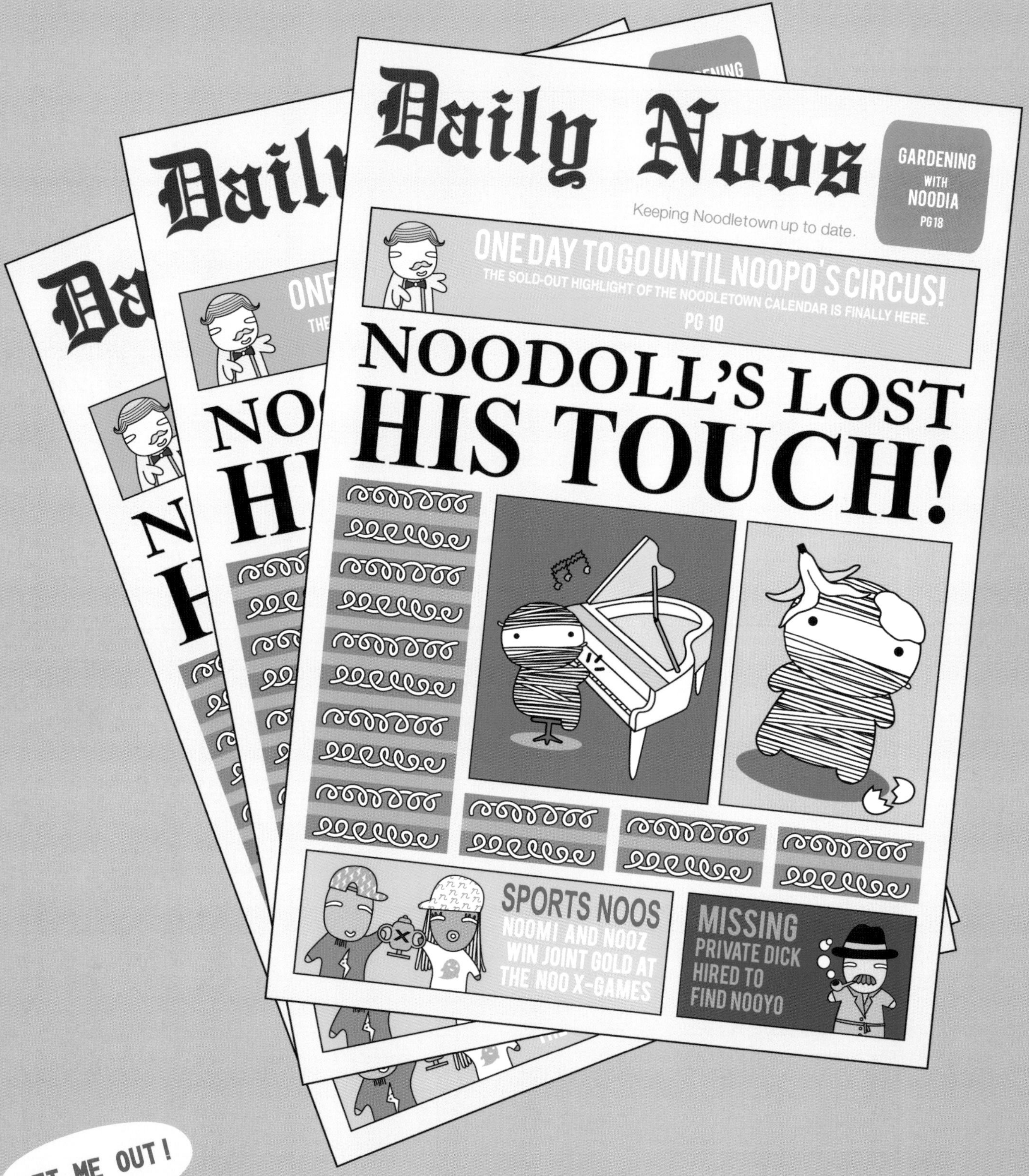

Daily Noos
GARDENING WITH NOODIA PG 18
Keeping Noodletown up to date.
ONE DAY TO GO UNTIL NOOPO'S CIRCUS!
THE SOLD-OUT HIGHLIGHT OF THE NOODLETOWN CALENDAR IS FINALLY HERE.
PG 10
NOODOLL'S LOST HIS TOUCH!
SPORTS NOOS
NOOMI AND NOOZ WIN JOINT GOLD AT THE NOO X-GAMES
MISSING
PRIVATE DICK HIRED TO FIND NOOYO


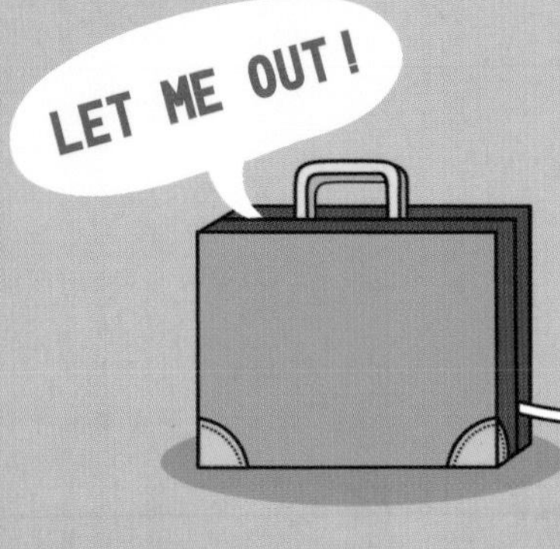

LET ME OUT!


But Ricehead cannot dance or sing.

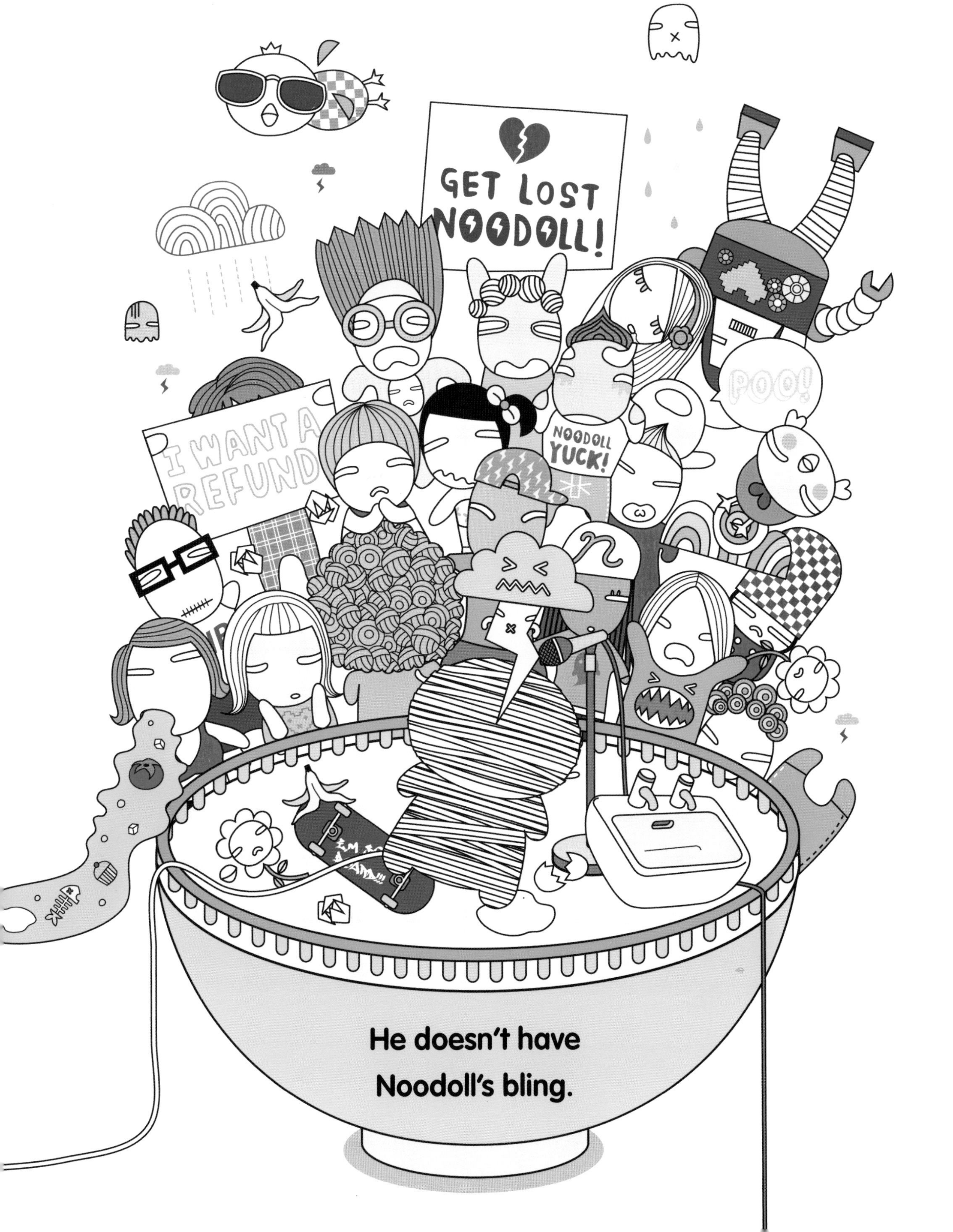
GET LOST NOODOLL!
I WANT A REFUND
NOODOLL YUCK!
POO!

He doesn't have Noodoll's bling.

When the circus comes to town,

Richead tries to be a clown.

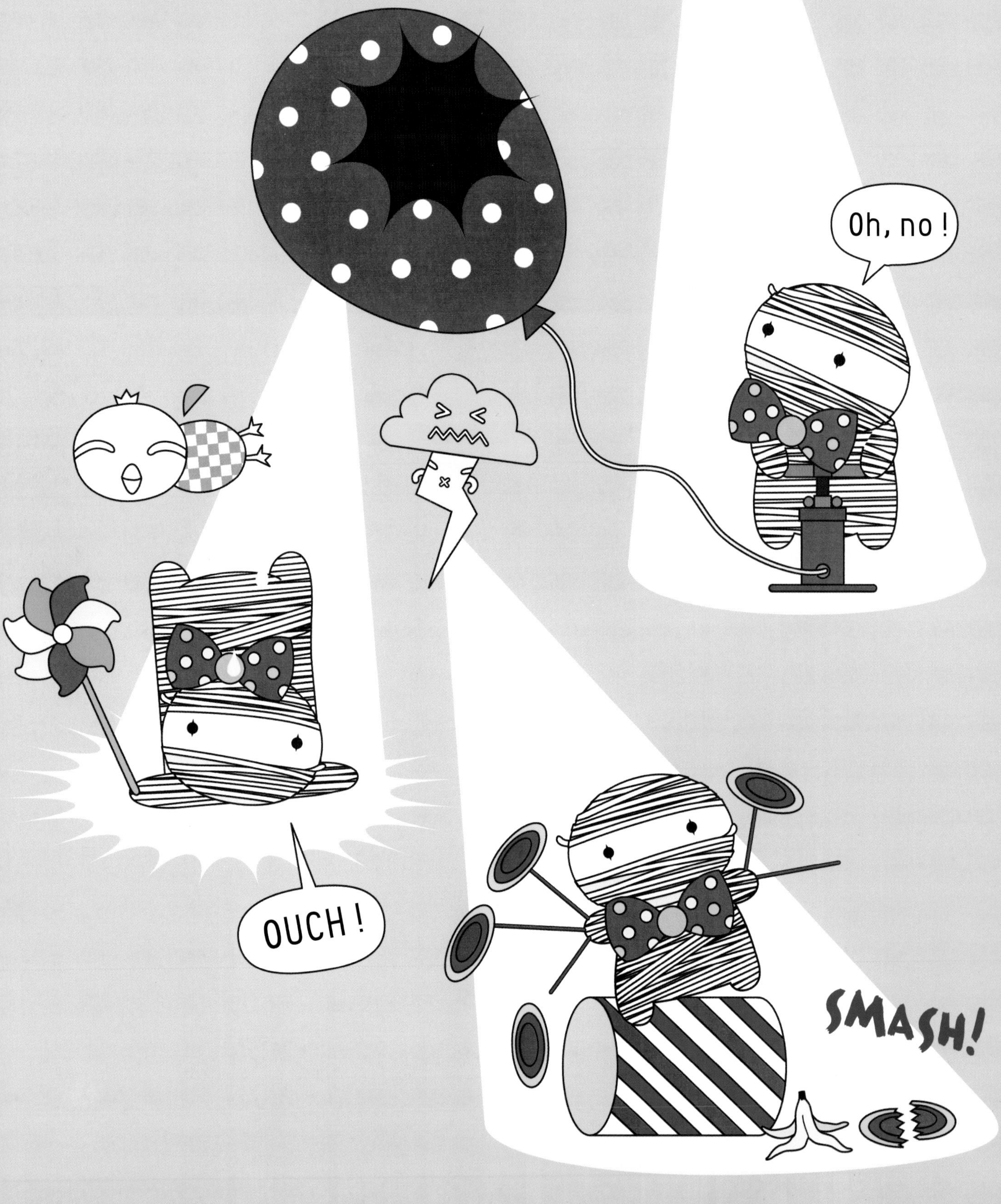
Oh, no !
OUCH !
SMASH!

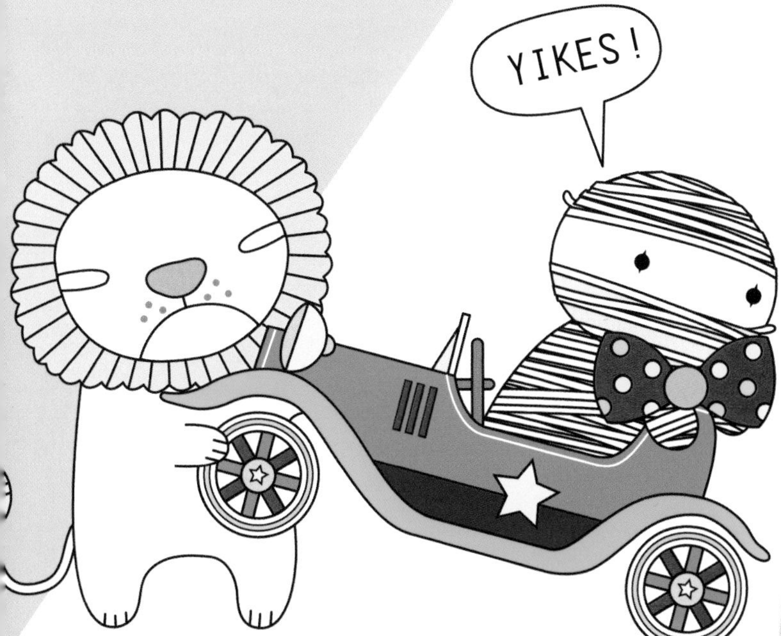
YIKES!

He crashes the bikes.

He drops the ball.

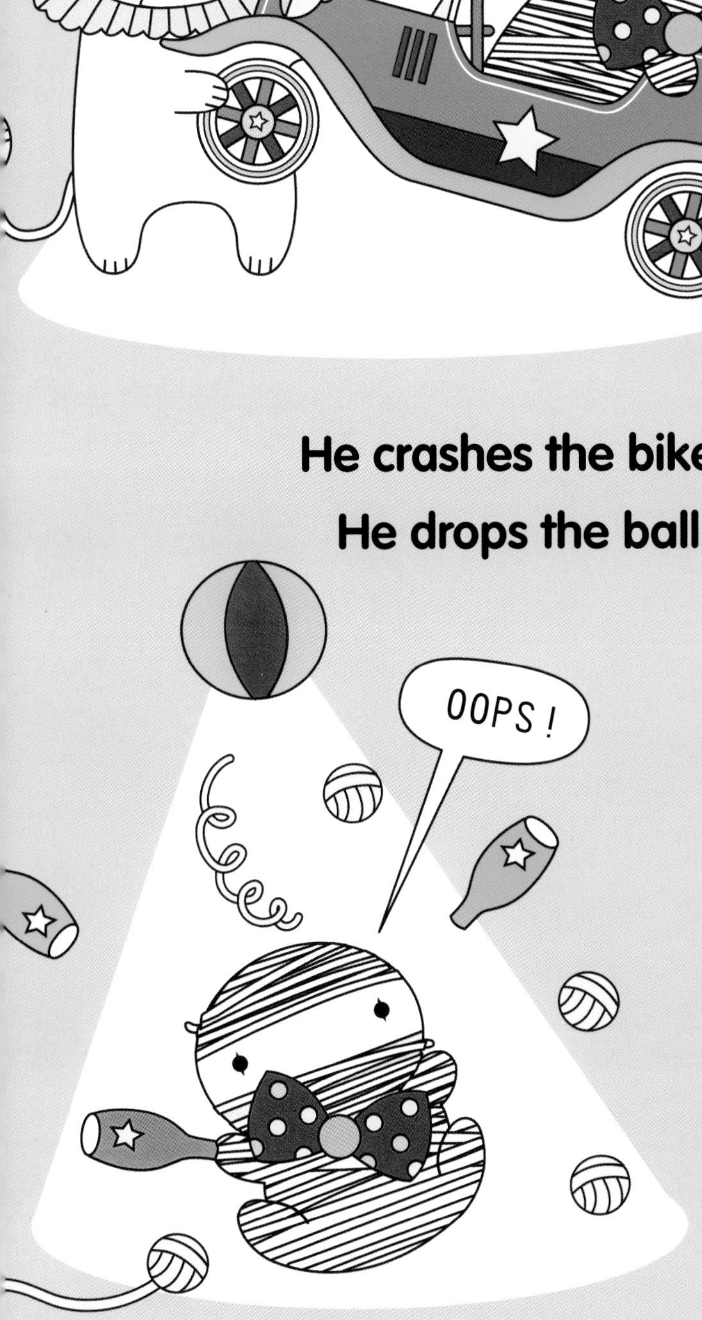
OOPS!

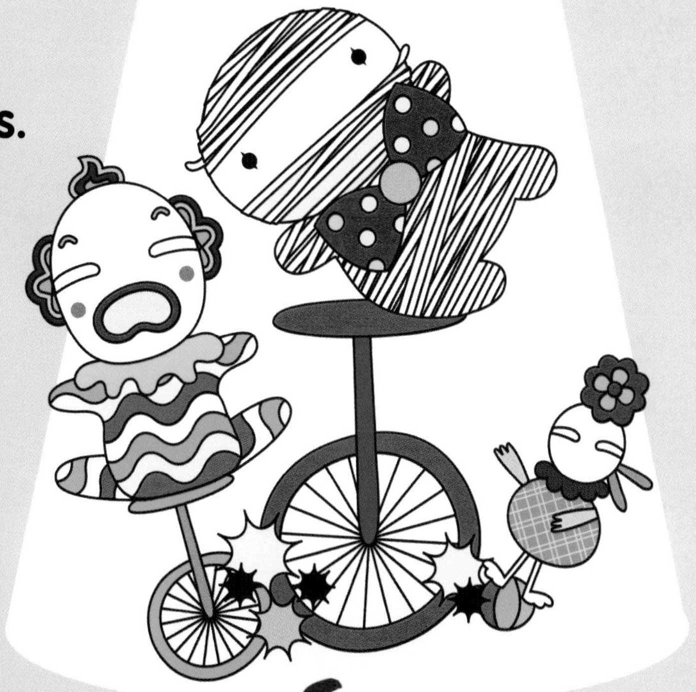
CRASH!

No one cheers for him at all!

**Everyone starts to hiss and boo.**
**What happened to the star they knew?**

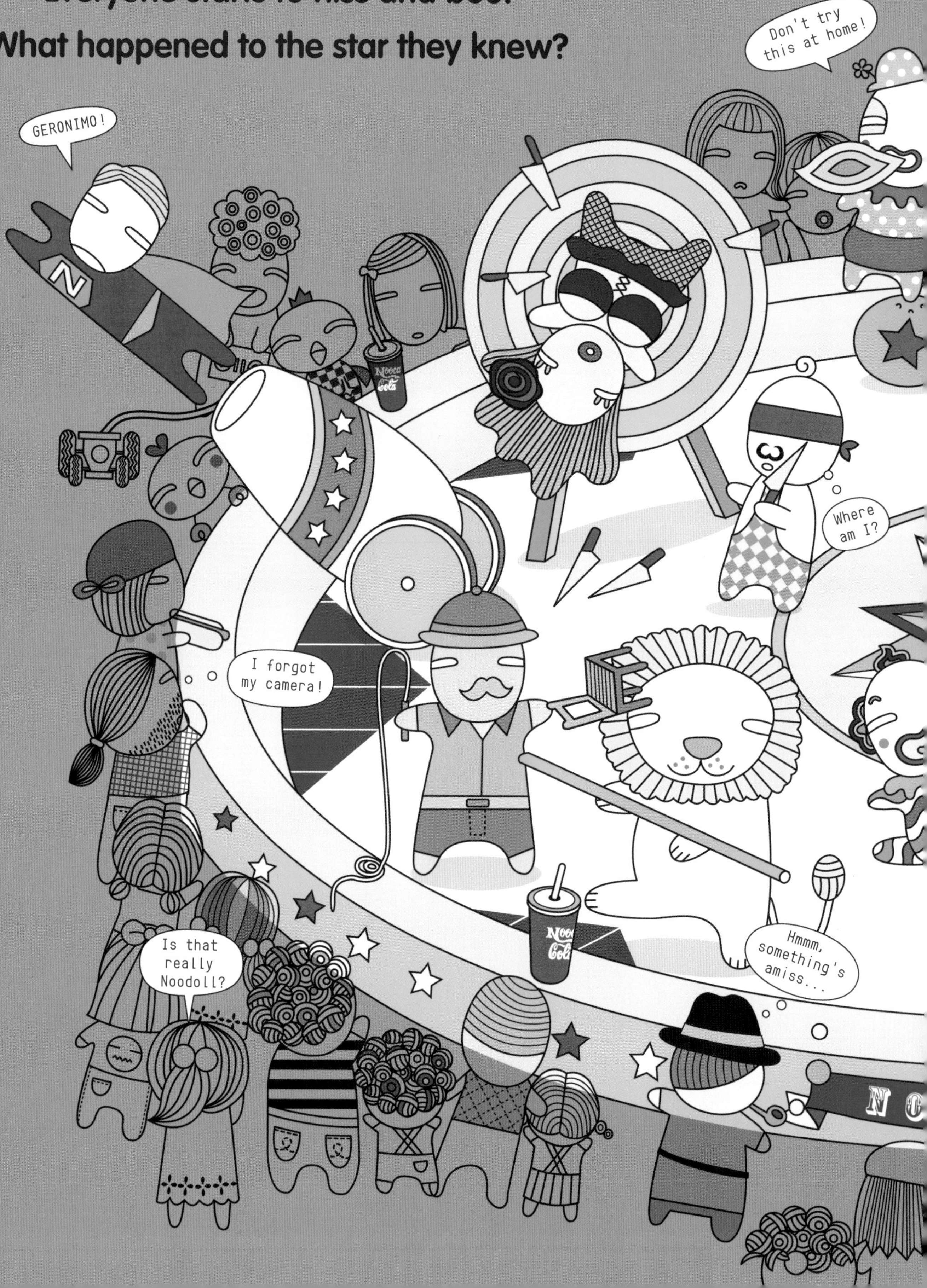

Don't try this at home!
GERONIMO!
Where am I?
I forgot my camera!
Is that really Noodoll?
Hmmm, something's amiss...

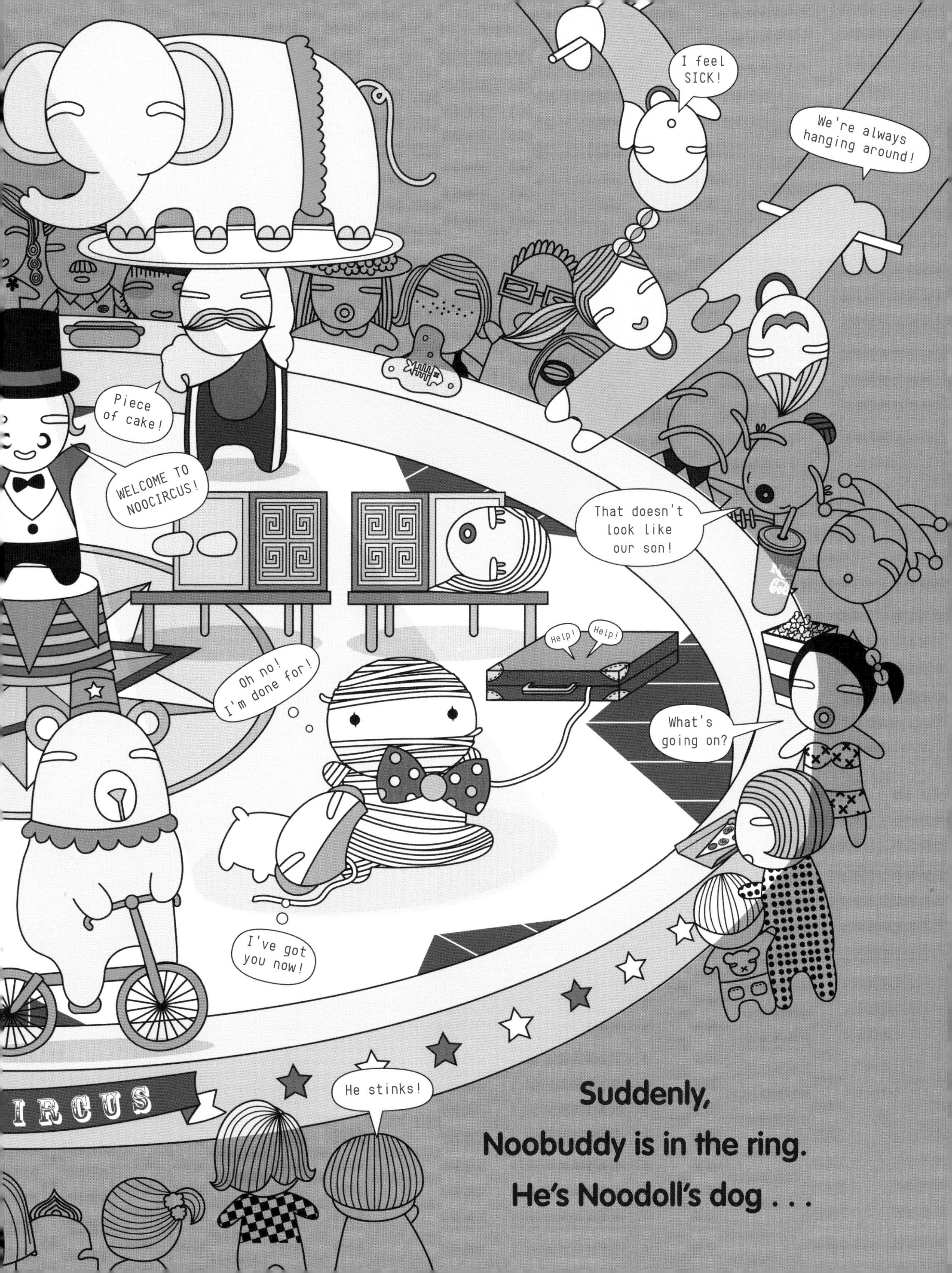
I feel SICK!
We're always hanging around!
Piece of cake!
WELCOME TO NOOCIRCUS!
That doesn't look like our son!
Help!
Help!
Oh no! I'm done for!
What's going on?
I've got you now!
He stinks!
IRCUS

**Suddenly,**
**Noobuddy is in the ring.**
**He's Noodoll's dog . . .**

. . . his bite has zing!

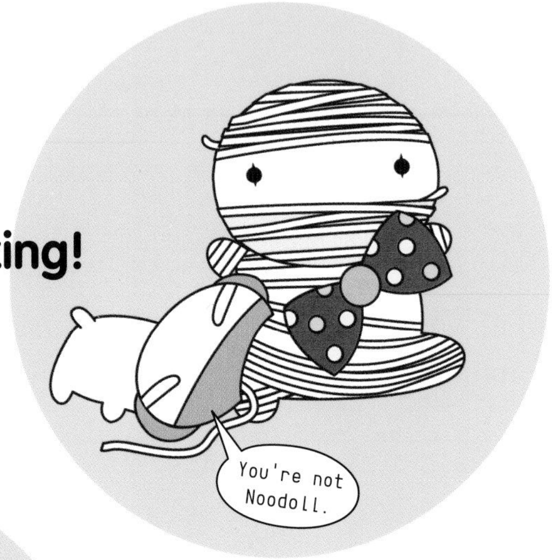
You're not Noodoll.

Ricehead whirls!

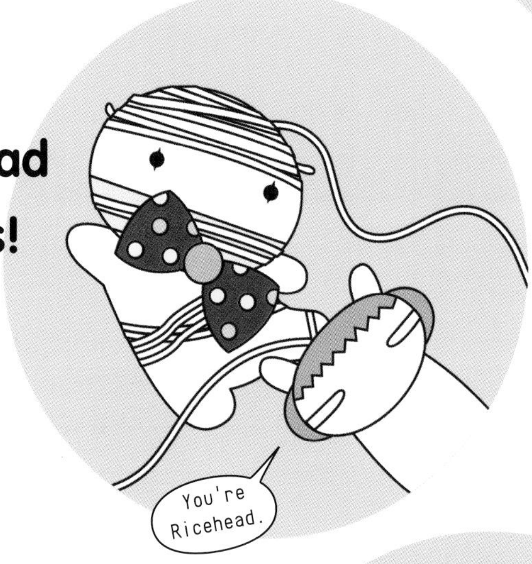
You're Ricehead.

He turns!

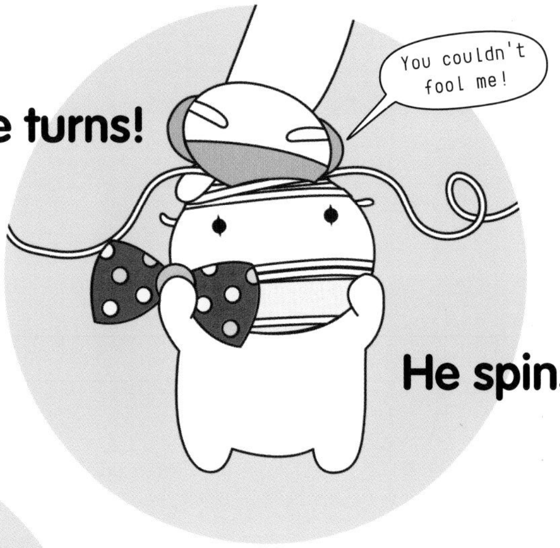
You couldn't fool me!

He spins!

The crowd gasps!

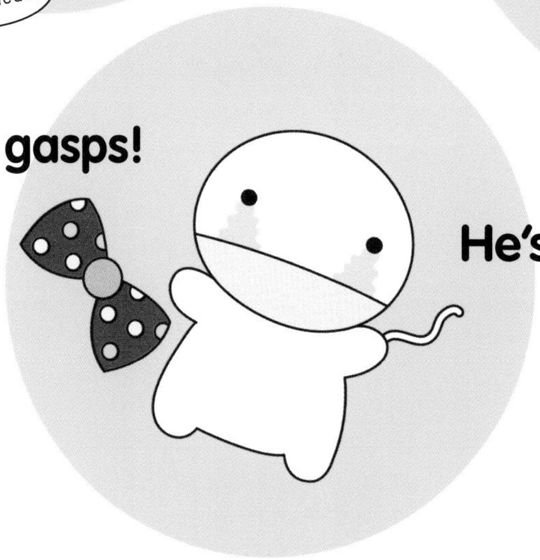

He's in Noodoll's skin.

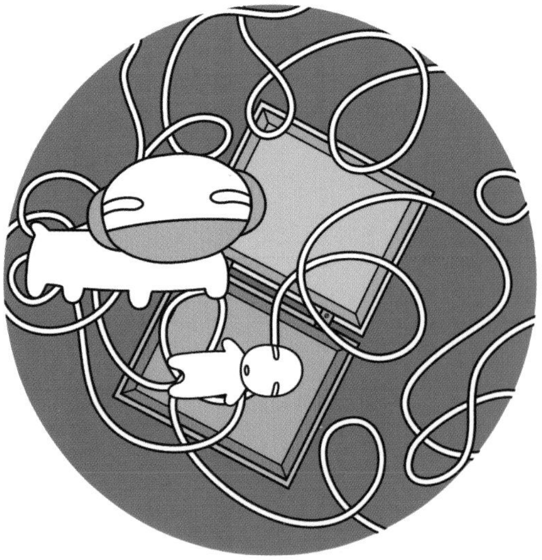

Noobuddy saved his friend at last.
Noodoll needs help, and needs it fast.

To his rescue comes the crew,
who act just like all best friends do:

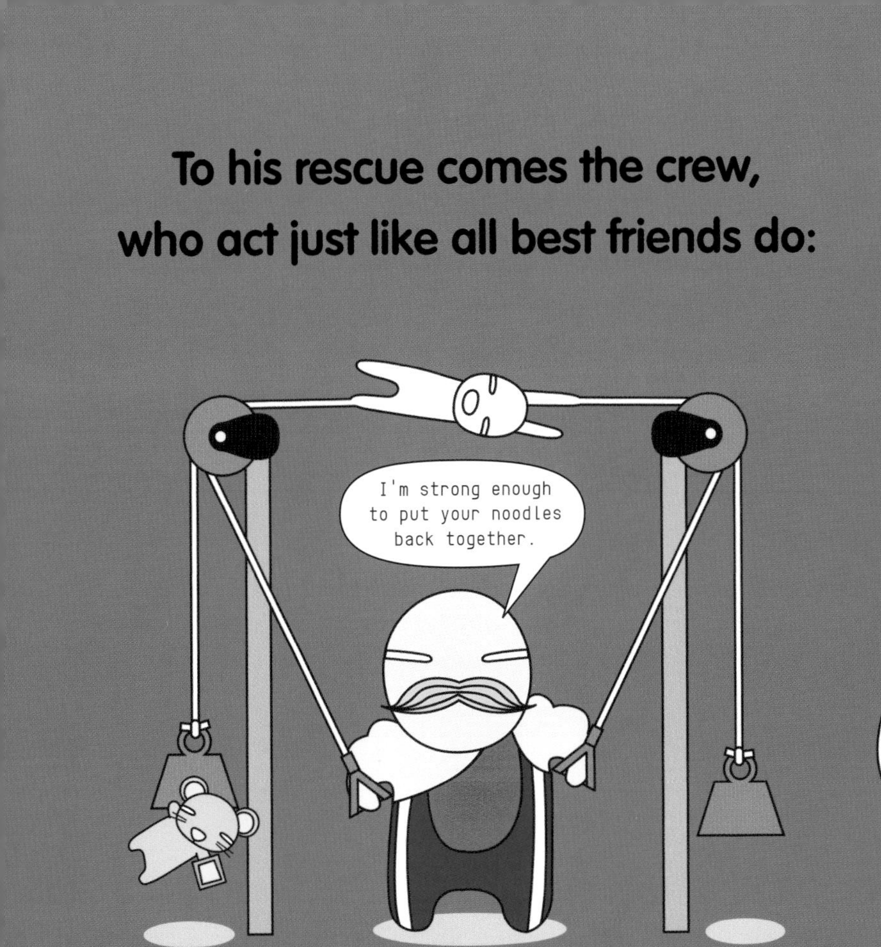
I'm strong enough to put your noodles back together.

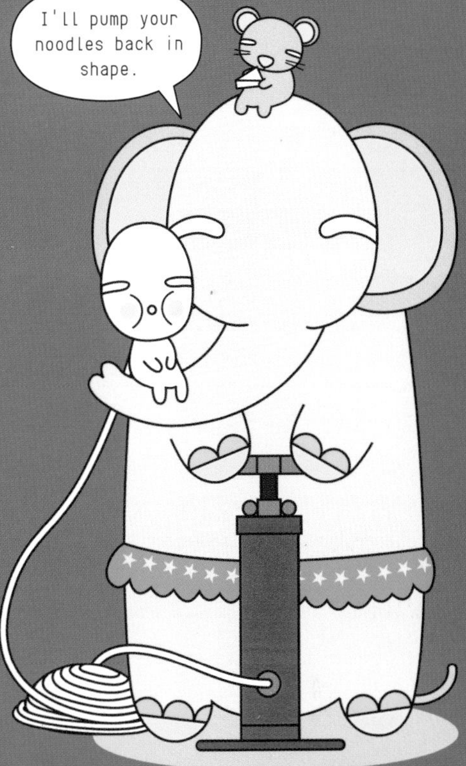
I'll pump your noodles back in shape.

They twist, they toss,
they smooth each crease.
Finally, Noodoll's in one piece!

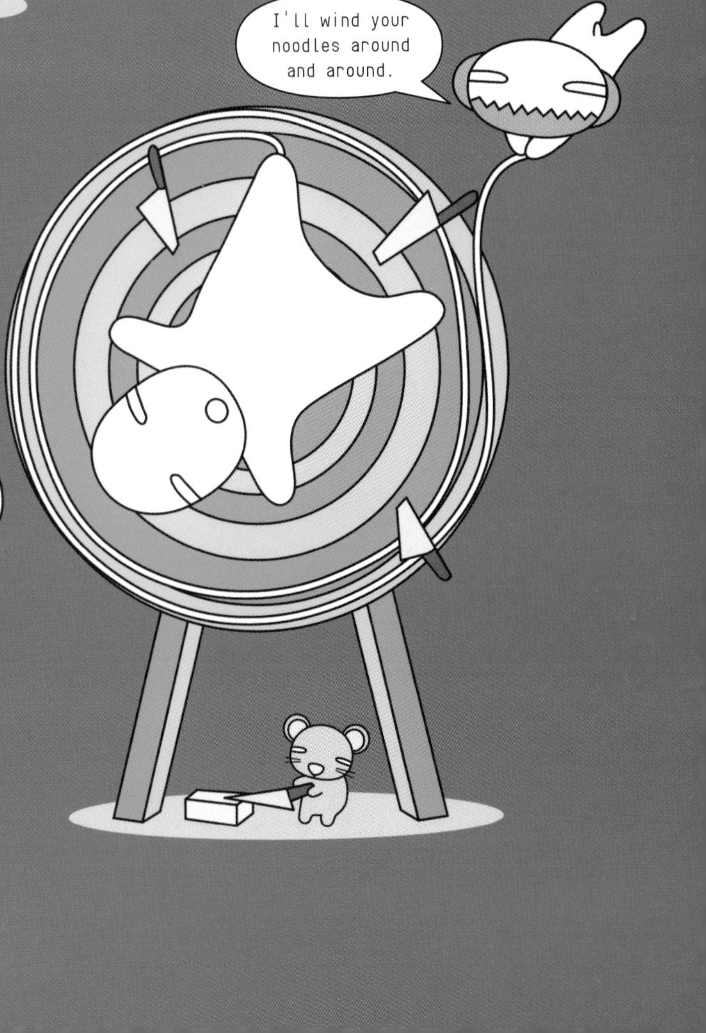
I'll wind your noodles around and around.

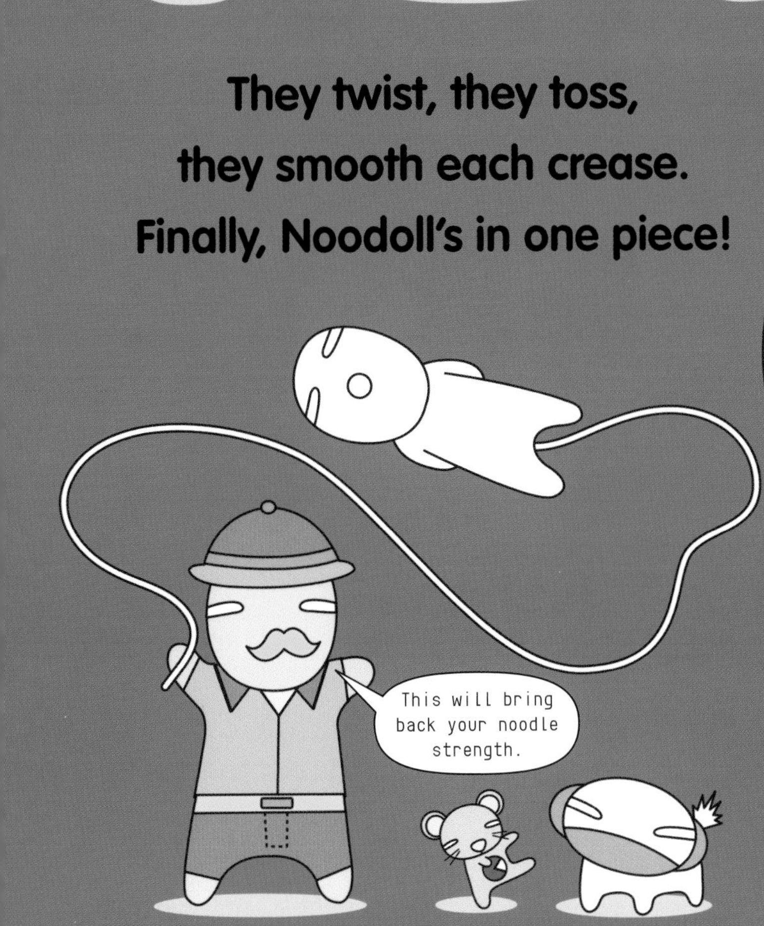
This will bring back your noodle strength.

Although Ricehead wasn't nice,
Noodoll offers this advice:

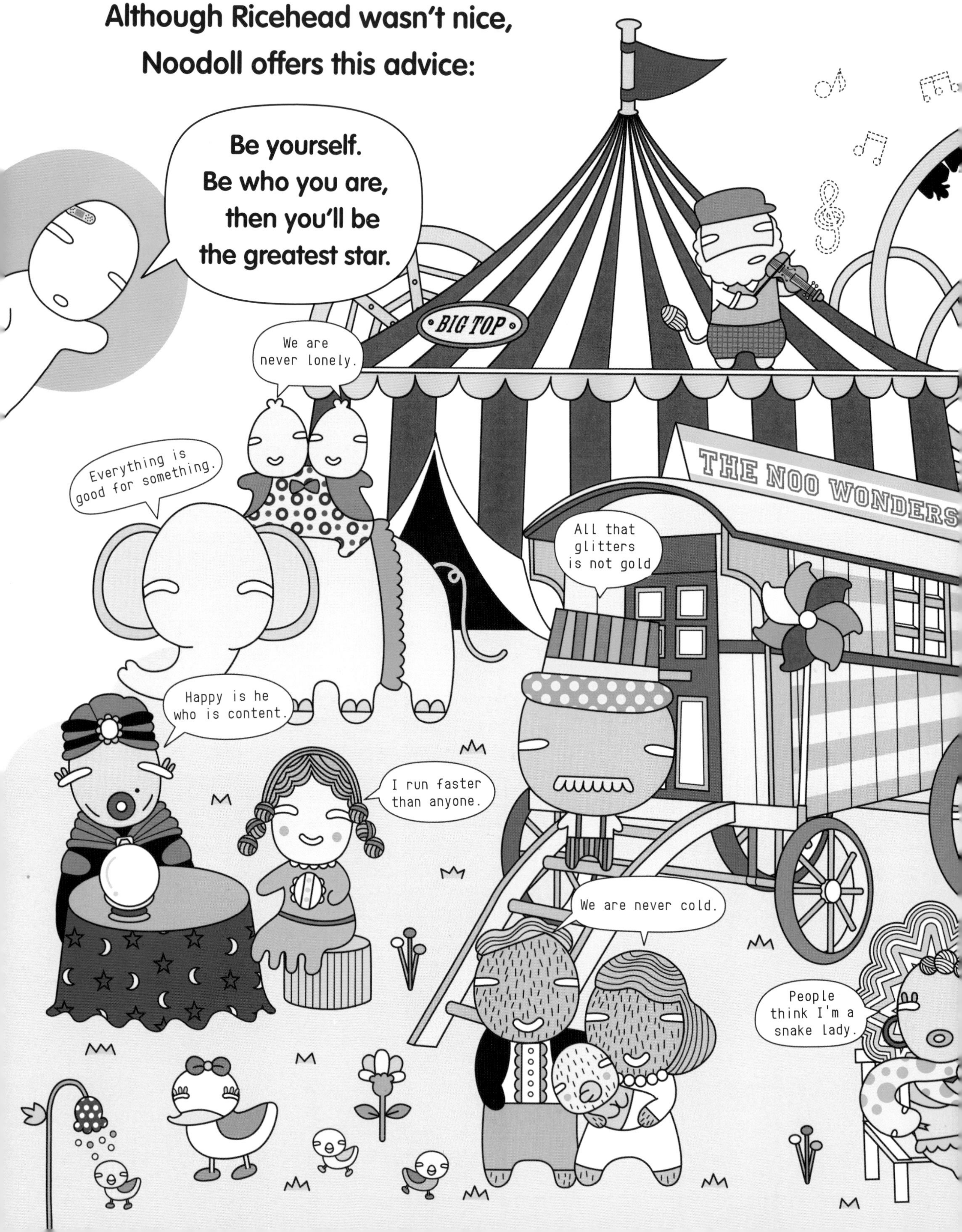
Be yourself. Be who you are, then you'll be the greatest star.
BIG TOP
We are never lonely.
Everything is good for something.
THE NOO WONDERS
All that glitters is not gold
Happy is he who is content.
I run faster than anyone.
We are never cold.
People think I'm a snake lady.

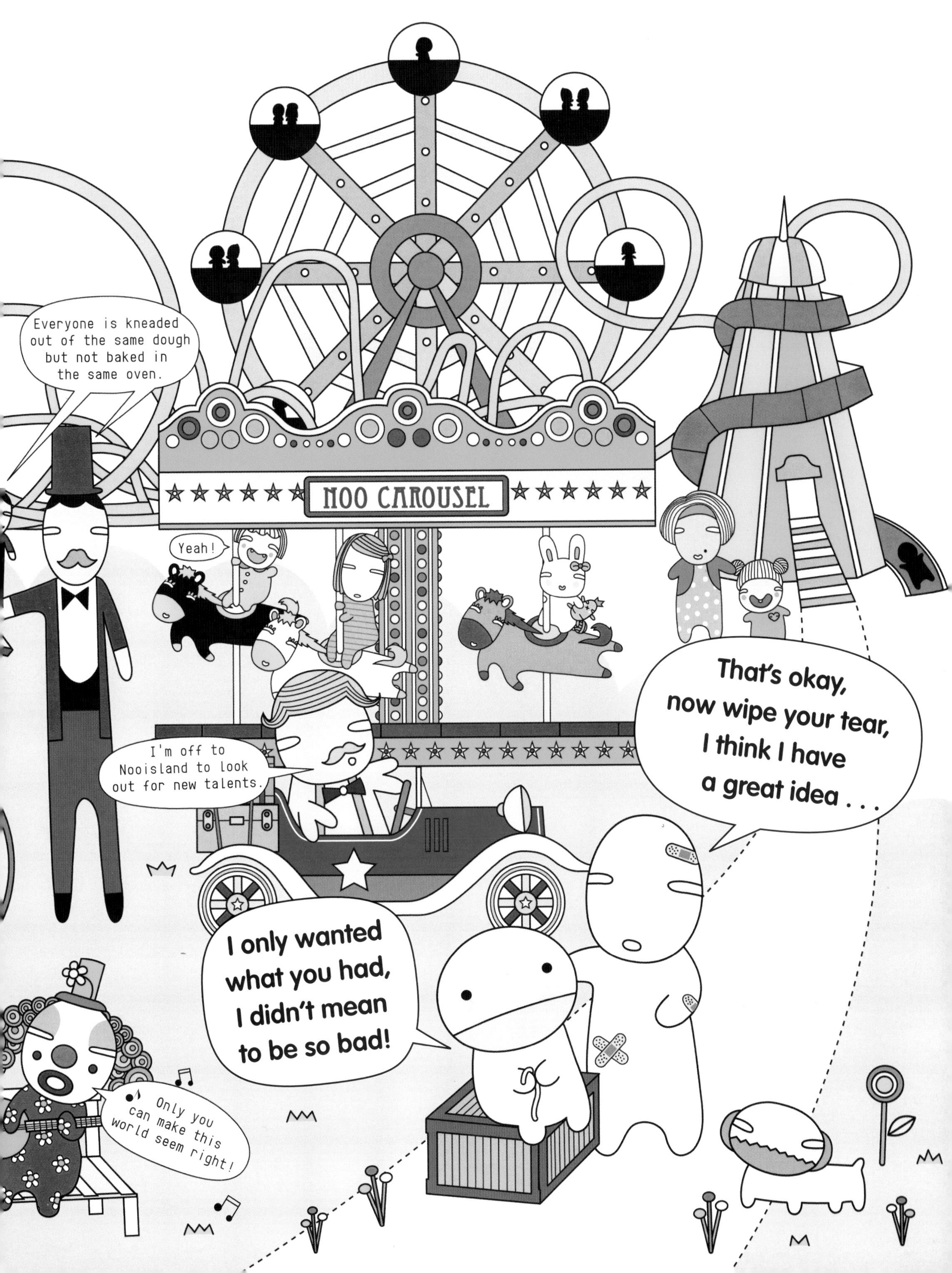
NOO CAROUSEL
Everyone is kneaded out of the same dough but not baked in the same oven.
Yeah!
I'm off to Nooisland to look out for new talents.
That's okay, now wipe your tear, I think I have a great idea . . .
I only wanted what you had, I didn't mean to be so bad!
Only you can make this world seem right!

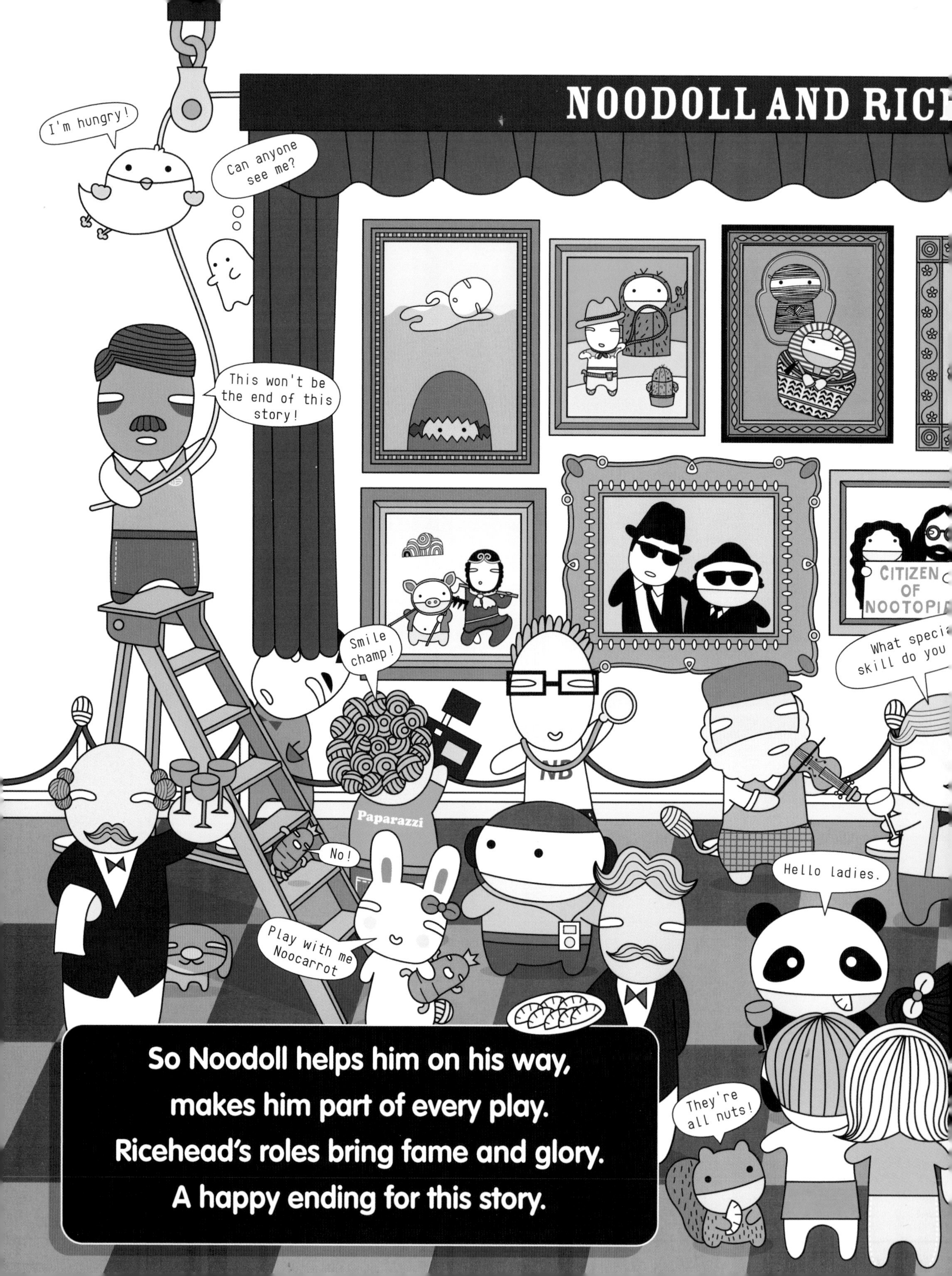
NOODOLL AND RIC
I'm hungry!
Can anyone see me?
This won't be the end of this story!
Smile champ!
CITIZEN OF NOOTOPI
What speci skill do you
NB
Paparazzi
No!
Hello ladies.
Play with me Noocarrot
They're all nuts!

So Noodoll helps him on his way,
makes him part of every play.
Ricehead's roles bring fame and glory.
A happy ending for this story.

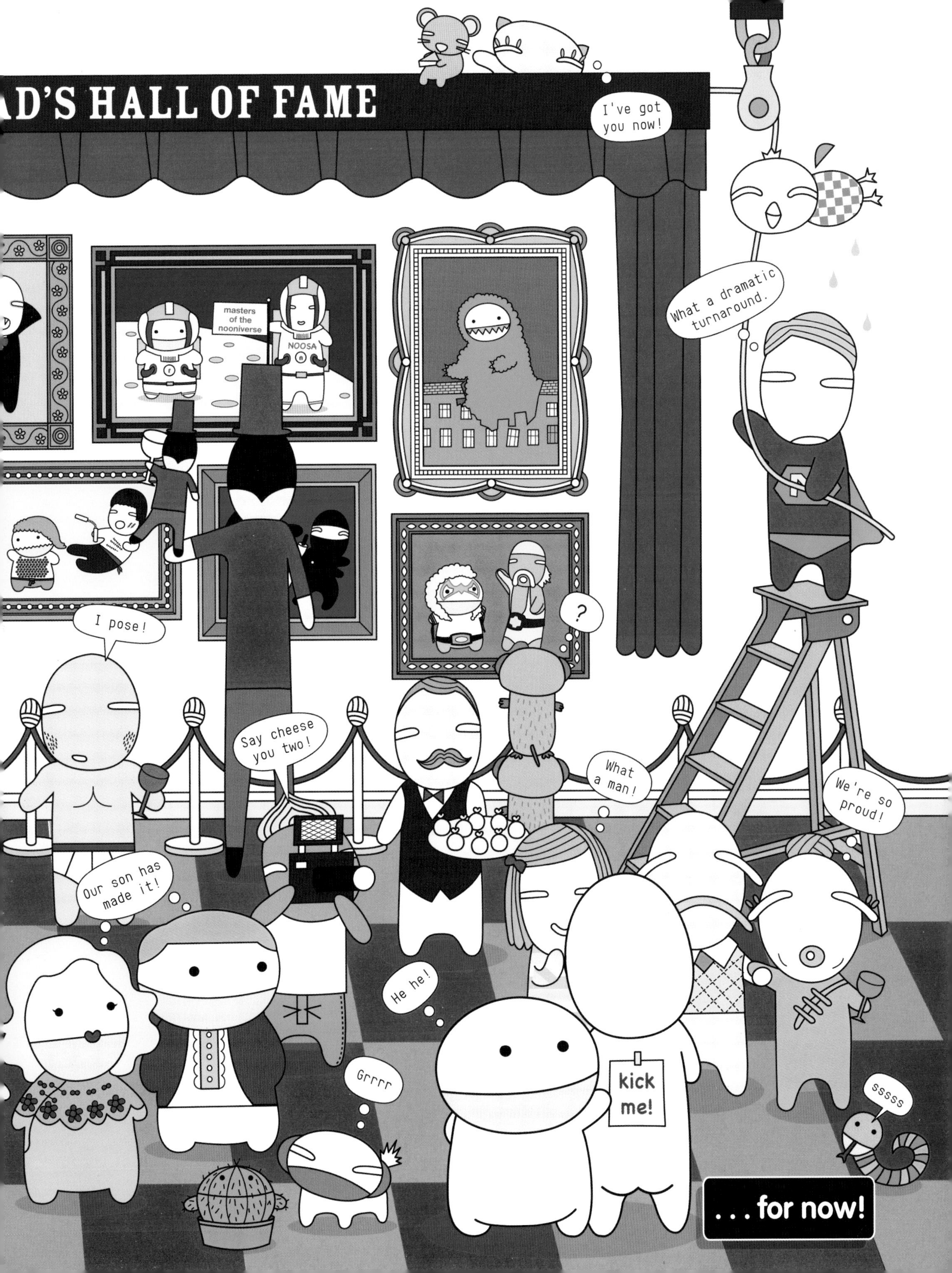

...D'S HALL OF FAME
I've got you now!
masters of the nooniverse
NOOSA
What a dramatic turnaround.
I pose!
?
Say cheese you two!
What a man!
We're so proud!
Our son has made it!
He he!
Grrrr
kick me!
sssss
. . . for now!

**Each Rice-Towner is somewhere in this book.**

**Can you find them all?**

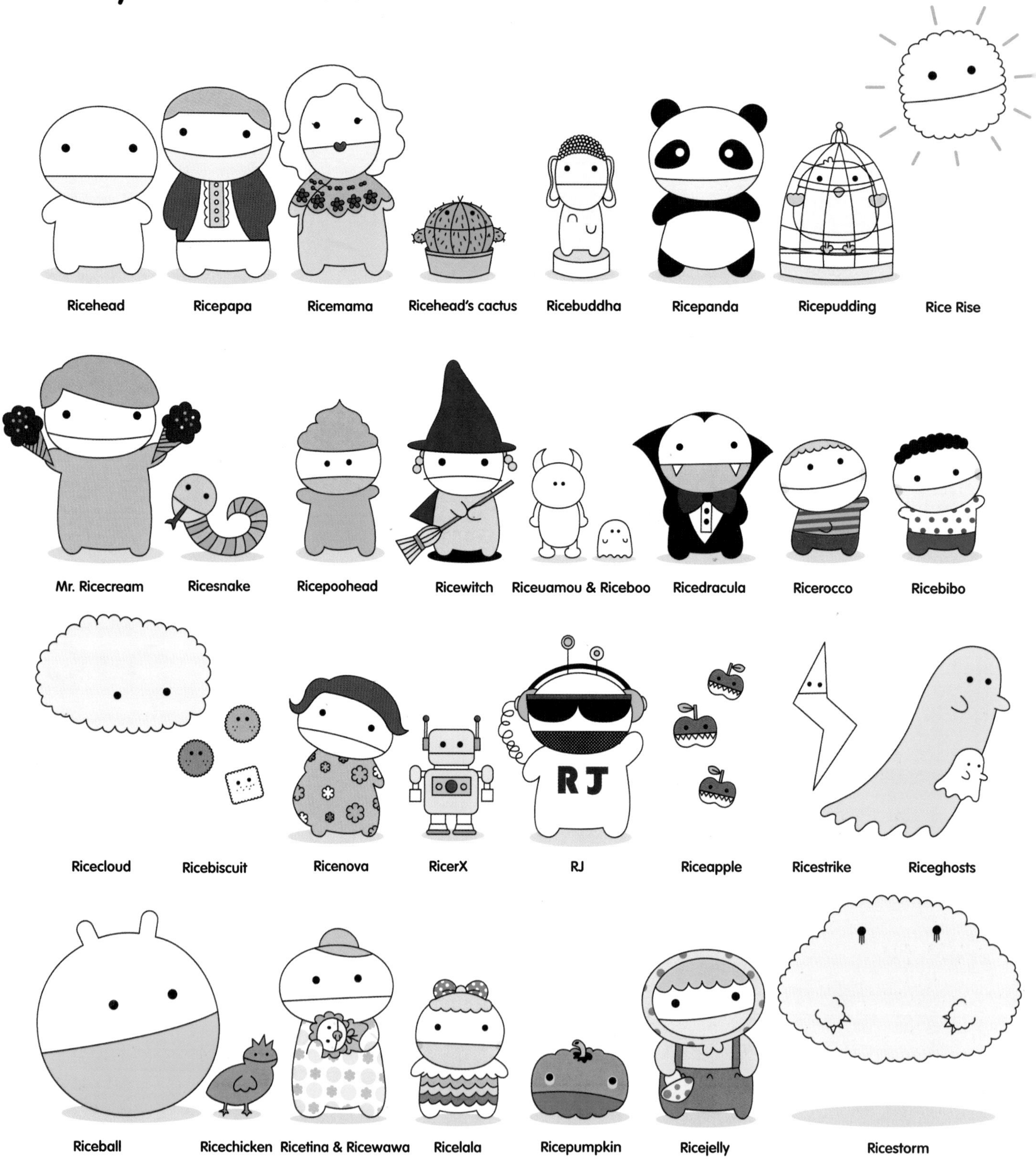
Ricehead
Ricepapa
Ricemama
Ricehead's cactus
Ricebuddha
Ricepanda
Ricepudding
Rice Rise
Mr. Ricecream
Ricesnake
Ricepoohead
Ricewitch
Riceuamou & Riceboo
Ricedracula
Ricerocco
Ricebibo
Ricecloud
Ricebiscuit
Ricenova
RicerX
RJ
RJ
Riceapple
Ricestrike
Riceghosts
Riceball
Ricechicken
Ricetina & Ricewawa
Ricelala
Ricepumpkin
Ricejelly
Ricestorm